EYE OF TIGER

TIGER

ROAR

JEAN MARIE RUSIN

Edited by N.Y.B.S and little tigers and
monkey, hyena, lions and leopard.

authorHOUSE®

AuthorHouse™ LLC
1663 Liberty Drive
Bloomington, IN 47403
www.authorhouse.com
Phone: 1-800-839-8640

Published by AuthorHouse 11/25/2013

ISBN: 978-1-4918-3878-5 (sc)
ISBN: 978-1-4918-3877-8 (e)

Dedicated to Katy Perry.

CONTENTS

CHAPTER 1

Joey and Karen decided to go to Africa for an adventure and Karen was not sure at first but Joey convince and they decided to go and sees tiger and monkeys and zebras and what would be great.

So they decided to fly there and sleep in tent and have a lot of camping and so Karen never when camping and she was a bit afraid.

Karen said going to a safari and I am sure that I am really for that type of vacation and we will be fine and don't worry, I will protection you.

About a month later they were on the plane to Africa for adventure safari trip that Joey was really thrill but Karen was scare for her life.

Joey said that when they arrive to Africa they will have a tour in the jungle of Africa and Karen said I would like to be in a five class hotel and in the jungle and Joey said that no fun, so where is your adventure? Not in the jungle said Karen, and Joey were waiting for the tour guide to show up and Karen said well I take a seat and it was really hot and humid and Joey said I think that I will take off my shirt and Karen said don't you might get in trouble.

So they waited and waited and then Leo shown up with his car and said we will be going about in ten minute, and Roy will comes along he is good with the jungle and you will be safe. Karen said I will stay at the hotel and he said don't chicken out you have fun and Karen said I don't think so.

Karen hesitates about it and then her when along with Joey and the tour guide and so they were off to the jungle and Karen was looking out of the window of the car and Karen saw Elephants and zebras roaming the land and Karen couldn't believe what she was seeing.

About two hour later, they reach there destiny and so Karen looks around and Joey said tonight we are going to sees the sky and the stars above.

I know that you will enjoyed very much and so they heard sound of the jungle and so Karen got close to Joey and said hold me tight.

About ten minutes later Karen fell asleep in Joey arms and Joey cover her up and left the tent and stayed out near the fire was burning.

Joey just sat there and the tour guide was sleeping and then Joey heard like a snake coming close to him and he somehow pull out the knife and killed the snake and Joey was glad that he did because otherwise he could have died.

The next morning Karen got up and she went out of the tent and looks around and she saw a tiger and she was about to scream but Joey said be quiet, it could attack us and she was silent and also afraid of her life.

Then the tour guide got up and said we have about 10 miles to go and you will see tigers and zebras and lions.

I am not sure that I want to sees that Joey, and Leo and Roy said you will not get hurt and Karen said how you know that we won't get hurt.

You could have hurt some anxiety in her voice and Joey said let have fun and you will be happy that you did.

Okay, I did agree to go on this safari and so I do the event and adventure with you Joey but if I feel that I am in danger, I will tell the tour guide to take us back, yes.

So they all when into the car and then they drove about five miles and they said now you to take your stuff and the rest of the ways we walks.

The further that they when the deeper into the jungle and Karen saw monkeys in the tree and they were swing back and forth and one monkey jump on Karen shoulder and Karen started to screams.

Joey said calm down and you will make the monkey bite you just stand still and Karen did and then the monkey just jump back to the tree and it was gone and Karen was relief.

About one hour later they were walking in the jungle and the wild hog ran toward them and Karen said I have enough and I want go back to civilization now.

Joey said it not going to hurt us and just keep on walking and so they kept for hour and hour and then they stop and the tour guide said tonight we will have camp here, here said Karen.

Karen said okay fine, and I am really exhaust and Karen was about to lay down and Joey heard a rattle snake and he shot it and Karen said, now what do I to be afraid of spiders…

But we will be fine and Karen said I am too tired to talk right and she put her head on the pillow and fell asleep and when to sleep.

But Joey was a bit restless and he got up and walks around.

CHAPTER 2

Then he came back to the camp and when back into the tent and Karen didn't know that he left. Morning came and Joey and Karen got up and the tour guide said is ready to go on the safari? Joey said yes of course and Karen was not sure what too says but they got there stuff ready, and they got into the car and the tour guide said make sure that you close your window, and it can be danger out here. And Karen said I thought it were safe, just be caution and safe said Leo and Roy agree, and Karen and Joey sat back and looks out the window the first view that saw was a pack of elephants roaming the field and about two of them were drinking water, and then they saw an giraffes and they were very tall and Karen took an picture of them and Karen couldn't believe what she was seeing for the first time and she was smiling at Joey and said I am glad that I came to Africa for vacation.

Karen and Joey were in South Africa and the landscape, and climate and the culture in West Cape around Cape town beautiful wine lands and mountain, and beaches to explores said Roy too Joey and Karen.

Roy asked do you wants to go to the beach and lay in the sun and Karen said no, I do not to do that right now, I just want to enjoy the fresh air and sees the animals. Soon you will so I need to warn you it can be dangerous.

I know but came to Africa to go on a safari and so I wants too sees, fine miss in a moment you will, okay.

We came to Africa for the habitats and remarkable of wildlife, yes we hear what you are saying.

Well miss most obvious is the attractions are the larger lions and leopards, elephants, giraffes, zebras, and I cannot wait to see that's! Well you saw some elephants, few minutes ago, yes that is true…

Joey said I would like to see the waterfall, and looks around, we will do that's!

Karen was just having her head on his shoulder and like falling asleep and Joey said yours going to missed it and don't sleep now, fine.

Then they stops and they all got out the car and they looks around and then suddenly they sees a white tiger in back of them and Karen said now what?

I don't know but be silent and it will go away and Karen said I am afraid and it might attack us and don't says that we will be fine.

About ten minutes the white tiger just walks by and then they all got into the car and drove away and that was a close called, yes it was.

Now it was getting later and Roy said we not continue today but we will set up a campsite and we will sleep under the stars, and tomorrow morning we will continue the safari and Karen said went are going to the hotel, not yet honey about three days from today, looks at our adventure, well I don't want died out here, you won't don't worry we will be fine here…

The night was quiet and they all fell asleep and then they hears a sound of an hyena and Karen woke up and said it could attack us, no it won't.

Some having those panic attack and you need to relax, I will but I will be better when the safari will be over, it will be but where is your adventure, Karen?

About half hour later Karen fell asleep and Joey got up and looks around and when back to bed and when into his sleeping bag and he felt something was crawling and it was an poisonous snake and somehow Joey had an knife on him and kill it and it was very close to him and

Roy ran in and said is everything okay? Yes it is… and Leo said well you're an lucky man, because you were be dead, please don't tell Karen about the snake, we will be running into a lot in the jungle and you need to warns her, you must tell her, I will.

Then Leo left into his tent and Joey went to sleep and the next morning came and Karen, it were nice to have an shower, well you will but not today.

About two hours later they left the campsite and drove off and then they drove and then they had an flat tire and the sun was strong and Karen was drinking a lot of water and said hope that we will soon leave, and Leo, in a bit we will leave. And then Leo notices that the gas was low. But was quiet about that's.

Karen asked Leo is everything okay and he shook his head and said yes we are fine but he was lying through his teeth and Joey didn't even think about asking about the car.

About two miles in the jungle, suddenly the car stops and Karen said why are we stopping? I think we are out of gas. What?

Now what? Well I call someone and they will location us and we will be fine.

I cannot believe what happening, Joey said we will get out the jungle and he will contact someone and then Leo said, I think the phone doesn't work.

Now Karen is really afraid and terrify and Joey hold Karen tight.

CHAPTER 3

Karen got out Joey arms and said it is all your fault that we are in the jungle and no one will save us, stops saying that Karen we will get out and we will not dies in the jungle and how do you know. Karen said did you tried your cell, it not working and we will get out here, and Leo said I will start walking back to town and I will come back with help and we will be stranded here alone, no Roy will be here and I think I better start walking and then Karen said how many miles to town and he answer about 3 to 4 miles and I should take too long and then Karen said about the hyenas, and Tigers and Lions, miss don't worry I have done this before and so everything will be okay, are you should yes I am.

Leo took his backpack and started to walks and walks and then he was not in the view anymore and Karen said, hope that make it okay.

Meanwhile Leo stops and then continue and then he hears something near the bushes and he stops and looks around and it is an baby cub, and he just keep on walking and now he feel that something is following him and once again stop and then it run out of the bush and tried to jump him and he just pull out the knife and killed it.

Back at the camp, Karen said well I think I will go inside the car and take an nap and Joey said well go on I will be outside for an while and Karen said don't be too long and he nodded his head and said I will be fine and Karen went inside and in the back seat and a pillow and then cover with an blanket and so Joey walks around and Roy advice Joey not to wander off and get lost and Joey said I need to pee and so Roy said be careful out there, I will…

Leo walk and walks but Leo a bit confuse and not sure where he is and then he walks into an pack of elephants, and now what/

Then slowly walks out and he hears shooting in the background and now he know there are hunters. And so Leo keeps on going and trying to get away.

But somehow he ran into the hunters and they tried not too let him go and first thing, "we cannot let you go" because you seen what we did.

So now Leo is begging for his life and Karen wake up and looks around and she is alone and she get out of the car and called out to Joey but nothing.

Then Roy said your friend just wander off and I was looking for him but I couldn't find him and Karen said don't leave alone here.

But I need to find your friend, I do understand and meanwhile and Joey got near the river and saw a small boat with some guns and then he just didn't know which ways to go back and so Joey when into circle and then he stops and saw an lions coming toward him and now Joey was in a panic…

Now Leo was being held like hostage and Karen was left behind with Roy and Roy said miss go back into the car and stayed there until I comes back with Joey and she said I am coming with you and he said no miss do what I says.

So Karen go back into the car and locked it and he don't let anyone sees you and I am saying that's for your protection.

Sure I will do what you says and I will be quiet and so he left her and walks into the jungle and somehow in finding Joey and he ended up in quicksand, and he was yelling and screaming for help but no one heard him and so Karen just stayed in the car and drank water and then she heard a bang and it was an tiger on top of the car and now Karen was afraid of her life.

Joey just stood frozen and didn't move and when he felt safe and started to move very slowly and then he walks around but didn't make a lot noise and then took a right and he heard someone calling for help.

Joey ran to that point and then saws Roy and Joey said I will get you out of there and then Joey found a big log and said move over a bit and I don't want to hit you.

About two hours later Leo somehow convince the hunters to let him go and so they drove him near Cape town and drop him off and he said thanks and just left in an hurried and they took off quickly and Leo when to the place where he work and got an jeep and filled it up with gas and drove off toward jungle and drove and drove and was not sure if he was going the right direction to Joey and Karen and Roy.

Leo stop and thought am I going the right ways and then he said to himself "yes I am and I will be there in two hours and but one thing that Leo forgot to sign for the jeep and then drive all the ways and then back to Karen was so frighten and scare and she just didn't move and then tiger left,

CHAPTER 4

Next morning Karen saw Joey and Roy and Leo all together and Karen got out the car and said, did you know that an tiger was on top of the car and you left me stranded to defend on myself, okay so get ready and we are leaving in five minutes and we are going abandon the car and we will go in this jeep and Karen said well I believe that the car was much safer than the jeep and he said it will be safe and don't worry about it Karen. Now are headed toward the river and Karen said "will be safe on the river" Leo said yes it will be and Joey said Karen you asking the man a lot questions, I just want to know and never been in Africa and never in a boat, so I need to know about our lives and seem like you don't asked and we are not in America and I need to know that we don't died here, okay, and then Joey said we are the first one that are taking an safari and so why are so afraid, I am not. So Leo drove and then they stops and they reach the river and now we need to go on the boat and Karen said okay.

Then Joey was joking around and said I will jump into the water and Karen said are you nuts and are you afraid that it could be infected, no I like adventure and not being an scary cat like you, stop this you getting me angry and spoiling our fun and trip when you acting like an jackass and stops calling me name and then she came out and saying you are an Mormon and I don't like that you are acting like an bitch...

About half ways in the river, they stop talking and Leo said don't put your hands in the water it will get bitten off and then the boat was about to tip and she said I don't want too died and Leo said we will not dies and we will reach land and the next stop will be mountains and you will be able to climb and Karen said I am afraid of height and you are making me climb a mountain, are out your mind and I didn't sign up for that. Do you hear what I am saying? Well honey you have no choice and you are going to climb that mountain and you will like it, and now Karen was getting furious and didn't speak with Joey.

Karen just didn't speak too Joey and Joey said "honey and don't be mad with me and we are having an adventure here, and then she nodded her head and said well okay, I will try it but I am somewhat afraid too.

Leo said we should be near where we are going to dock the boat and hike a bit to the mountain sight and you need to watched out for wild hog and they are really mean pigs that bite, okay.

They got out of boat and started to walk in the jungle and to reach the mountain they rain into the "Lion den" and they were surround and Karen was panic and Leo said don't run, be very quiet and then we will be fine.

Most of all don't looks into their eyes and then out the bushes there was a tribe with knife and coloring faces and Leo said well I think they will take us to there camp and I don't know what they will do to us.

Karen said this was the part of the safari? No, I think that we are in trouble and no one doesn't know that we are. Thanks a lot Joey…

I thought this trip was going get us closer but it will put us a part.

Don't says that Karen and I am very sorry to put you in this danger and so somehow the lions didn't attack and so the tribe point arrows and knives and they had to follow them and Joey, just had an gut feeling when they arrival to the camp, but Joey and Karen didn't know this was a part of the safari and they were going to get harm and then, they told them to sit down and then music started to plays and one of them brought them bananas and Karen was not sure if she should eat it and then a lot monkeys started to jump at them and then one of the girl of the tribe started to dance and she was half naked and dark skin with black hair and earring in her ears and nose and then few children came around and started to touch Karen and her long blonde hair and blue eyes and then they touch Joey with the black hair and the mustache and a little gray on the side and the half naked lady asked Joey to dance and so he got up and dance with her and then they spoke an foreign language and then Leo said, they are the part of safari and so, why didn't tell us and I frighten to death, no need Karen and you and your boyfriend will be fine.

After the show, they were shown to their tent and Karen said Joey, you told this were be an adventure and it is different but I cannot wait to get back to the hotel, come on Karen will hear you whiny on this trip, no you won't.

Later that night Joey tried to make love and Karen said not here at the hotel maybe, now you acting like a bitch.

She pulls the cover and turns around and didn't face Joey that night and then the rain started to pour.

So Joey was restless and he got up and sat to the half- naked lady and she started to speak in English and then she said I have two boys.

But the lady said my man will get angry, okay!

CHAPTER 5

When are they were leaving but they still being follow and so Karen said I thought this was part of safari, it was but they are very protection tribe and but I cannot explains too you, miss, fine…but stayed very close to me and don't take any pictures, then they might attack, okay so I will put the camera away and I will walk very slowly and we can leave, so is that the plan? Yes and so Joey and Karen and Leo are there way out of the bushes jungle and so Karen was relieve that the tribe are not going after them and Leo said go right to the boat and we will leave immediately, okay and Joey was behind Karen and they were not too far from the boat and Leo was speaking there language and Joey and Karen said "will he be all ready"? Yes I believe he will…

About half hour later Leo came and said go into the boat now and we need to leave now, and then the tribe somehow charges out and was going after them and arrows were shot and miss them by an inch.

Now Karen is very scare and frighten they were going up river and they saw sees alligators in the water and Leo says don't make a sound.

The water is mudding and it is not clear and I don't sees it and it not too far from us and be silent, okay I will.

Joey said the alligators know that we are in the water and then Leo said, I just saw a big snake in the river and I need to paddle faster and the water is infected with snakes and alligators and I don't want to be here. Soon we will be back on land. Good then Leo said we will light up the fire and we will camp out in the jungle and well you need to know a lot poisonous spiders and bugs that I need to warns you, fine.

Then Karen said why did you bring me here? Well you always complain about having an adventure, so we are having one.

I don't like being in the jungle and then a cheetahs came over and pull something out her bag and Karen yelled out and said bring back and Karen got up and Leo said Let it be, Miss. No I need it and I have to get it back, you will never catch up and I, advice not to go and you will be sorry if you do.

About a minute later bat hang over there head and Karen said we cannot sleep here when the bats are over our head and they will wake up and attack us.

Once again Leo said sit down miss and don't make any emotion and they are waking up and now what? They will attack us, no they will not…

About one hour later they when to sleep, some tribe came to the camp and Karen woke up and some tribe man was staring at her and she was afraid to scream but she shook Joey and he somehow woke up and said what do you wants? And she said look up and I don't tell you.

About a minute later, Leo was surrounding by the painted tribe with arrows and knife and half naked women of the tribe and babies, stand above them.

Leo started to speak and one tribe man push him to the ground and tied him up and then they drag Karen and Joey out and then they took them to there camp and they were tied to the poles and Leo was trying to say, let us go and then the rain came and they were soaking wet and Karen notice they were a cannibal tribe and they will be the meal for them., and Karen said we need to escape and if we don't we will be there meal. I know miss, and why did take us here?

I thought it was safe, and the pot was boiling and smell like bones and about one minute the chief of the tribe came out and said let them go…

He recognized Leo and let them then goes and Leo and Karen and Joey were free and Leo said head to the boat and we are leaving this place now.

Once again they got into the boat and they when up river and it was really rapidly and fast and at that moment Karen thought she were fall out of the boat into the river with infect water with alligator and croc, and snakes that would swallow you in a minute.

They got in the other side of the river and they were near the mountain side and now they will be climbing the mountain and Karen said I don't sees anything and this is night we set up camp and Leo said not here.

I don't understand, you set up camp here, you will be attack by a white tiger or leopard, I am too exhausted to climb, but you must climb to live…

Now Karen was angry and hungry and she didn't speak to Joey and Joey tried to help her and she refuse and then Leo gave his hand and help her up and she said thanks!

They were on top of the mountain and Karen just stayed away from Joey and Joey came closer and said I am sorry about the trip and when we get home, hope that you will forgive and I just wanted to get closer.

Well seem like that we are getting further of this adventure trip.

CHAPTER 6

Joey was trying to get closer too Karen and Karen said I want to be left alone.

Come on Karen, we need to talked and thing will work out and I know that you still love me and I love you.

I guess we should decide on the adventure but I just book this trip and I thought you would love it but I was wrong, sorry and he tried to kiss her lips and she push him away and when into the tent alone and Joey sat with Leo and talked with him and he said well your girlfriend seem to be angry at you and then Joey said soon I hope that the safari will be over too.

In two day and then we will be back in the hotel, yes. But Joey sat at the camp fire and said so what are going to eat and Leo said well we will have some fish and green leaves and so Leo prepare it and Joey said I am starving and I really need to filled up stomach. But eat slowly and okay and Joey took a bottle water and swallow. Karen got up and came to eat dinner and Joey said sit down next too me and so she did.

But don't touch Me., fine and she ate some foods and water and when back to sleep and she said don't you comes in I don't want to be next too you right now. I don't want you around me right now.

Joey said why are you acting this ways and it shouldn't make any different and we will be in the hotel in two days and we will not get hurt and how do you know that we won't? Come to me and let me close tonight and Karen said no I want to be alone and she when into the tent and close it and about ten minutes she screaming and said there is an snake and Joey run in and it almost bit him and somehow Joey chase the snake way and Karen get close for an second and said now you can leave and about the snake might comes back.

Joey step out and he hears an rattle and sound and it kind of jump on his leg and he fall down and Leo run and stab the snake and it dead and he goes and help Joey and take out the poison and spite it out of mouth and Karen comes out and run up to Joey and said what Happen to Joey and Leo Explains and then she goes closer and give him an hug and asked Leo will Joey will be all right? He said I am not sure because I am not sure how much poison that he got inside of him and he is running a fever and it might be touch and go!

No he cannot die, you need to save him, watched out there are many snakes in the jungle and they are much bigger than the rattle, I do understand but save him, don't worry miss, if he live to the morning he will live.

Karen stayed with Joey all night and listen to his heart and sees if he was breathing and Leo was watching out for leopard and tigers and lions and so Leo looked around and didn't sleep all night and Karen fell asleep and then Leo woke her and said he will be fine and don't worry.

But Karen was little worry and wanted to apologize to Joey but he was sleeping like in an coma, but Karen put her head next to his shoulder and said I will leave you and you do mean a lot too me and I said those awful things when I was angry and so please god let Joey be fine.

Then the morning came and Joey woke up and said what happen and Karen didn't wanted to tell him and Leo about to tell him and Karen said don't tell him, I tell him later at the hotel, okay Miss.

Joey wanted to get up but he kind of weak to walks and then Karen help him up and took him into the tent and lay his head on the sleeping bag and he close his eyes and Karen stayed with him and Leo said we cannot stayed here we need to move now… Before night …

Karen said I don't if Joey could go on he must, it not safe here, why do you say that so about the snakes that are coming out that mean our wild animals will attack us if we don't move…

So Karen got her stuff and pack it and Joey too and they were ready to leave the mountain and go toward the beaches, but Leo was getting more confuse about direction and Leo didn't say that they were lost.

Probably more dangers will occurs and so Leo kept it to himself and Karen walks slowly down the mountain to the dirt road to reach the beach and Karen said we need to rest for five minutes, only five and then we need to go soon.

But Leo looks up the sky and said we need to go south about five miles and then we will reach the beach and meanwhile Karen was holding Joey and Joey almost fell to the ground.

Now Leo was headed toward the path and he said now we will be taking a right and then straight to the beach, and Karen said that sound good and I cannot wait.

Karen didn't notice anything strange but thought they were ahead to the beach and but a lot of jungle and tree and lot of monkey on the trees.

Once again they stop and Leo said one more time stop.

CHAPTER 7

Leo started to walk and then he fell into quicksand and calls out to Karen and Joey and you need to help me out and I am sinking, oh my god and Joey looks and said what are we going to do now? Don't worry Joey we are going to help Leo somehow and I don't but we will save him.

Are you sure? Yes I am and so you are going to help me and we will get some log and place them and some vines and somehow tied them and then Leo will be fine. How do you know this stuff Joey, I just do know it and we will have pull and make sure that he doesn't stink and stink and I heard what you saying and you don't fall into the quicksand no way and I know how to survive these kind of situation but you did get bitten by a poison snake and you almost die and so don't tell me that you know how to survive, are angry with me?

When we suppose to help Leo and now we are having a fight when this man could dead in ten minutes if we don't save him, and we need him to get us back to civilization and that truest so let work together and gets out of the jungle and get home and into an warm bed and having some strawberry and cream.

Karen said sure let do it and then we can head back to the boat and then we can go to the hotel and sleep in a conformable bed together, yes I agree...

About ten minutes later they pull Leo out the quicksand and he got clean up and heading to the path toward the boat and the safari was over and Karen was relieve about that's.

When they got to the boat and the boat was DAMAGE, and now what so we need to fix it and sail away, and so it make leak but we will be able to go down river and reach our destination, are sure Joey?

Yes, and Leo wanted to says it was a bit of risk but he kept quiet about journey back and so Leo was not talkative at that point and so they patch the boat and push the boat on the river and they all got in and sail down river and but the boat was leaking and it was not a good sign and Karen was really scare...

About half of the boat ride, It leak more and more and then it was stinking and Karen was panic and scare and so was Joey and Leo.

The moment that they when down river, that the boat broke in half and Joey grabs Karen and they swim to the shore and then Karen said where Leo is?

I don't know Karen but we are safe and we are not too far from the hotel and Karen, did you see him, no I think that he make it to the shore.

But he is not here, and then they looks around and then they saw him face down and then Karen ran up and pick him up but it was not too late and we need to get him help we will but we are not able to carry him so we will have comes back, you cannot leave him alone here, some wild animal will eat him but we have no choice do you understand what I am saying Karen, loud and clear. He probably drown and now we are stranded and we will not be able to get back and we will live in the jungle and about ten minutes Leo was laying on the sand and Karen said is he alive? I don't know and so he check his pulse and he said Leo is barely alive but we need to found someone, but we are on some land and I don't know if it is civilization and we can end up with cannibal peoples and they will have us for dinner, stop this whiny.

Joey I want to have a hot shower and lay in bed and watched some movie and then go back home and start our life, and be with you and now we are somewhere and known one is looking for us, and about the our tour guide.

Well he probably thinks that we are back at the hotel and so we are alone out here and Joey said don't worry we will be safe and we will be back home.

We might fall in quicksand but we are not we when on a river boat upriver and ended up on land and we don't know where we are?

I don't like it and we should have gone to Hawaii and so you pick Africa and now we somehow jungle and now on some beach and so I don't know what going happen but we are together and now and we will be fine…

Leo started to make sound and he wanted to get up but Joey said stay down and rest and then Joey noticed blood and he is bleeding, do you have something wrap it up and it will stop with the pressure.

Karen said when we get home, and the next vacation will be Hawaii and you promise that no more safari trip, I do.

Leo once again passed out and Karen said hope that he will be fine…

Don't worry babe, we will get home and then Karen said something is crawling up on me, and he said don't move…

What is it? Quiet it going to bite you, no it a snake, and he nodded his head and said I will killed it and Karen said don't let it bite you.

CHAPTER 8

Looks out Joey, it near you, I know and I am trying not get bitten and looks out one is coming near you and we need to move Leo now…

Yes, I feel that we are surrounded by snakes and they are poisonous snakes and that is not good and we need to carry him and we need not to snarl the snakes toward us and we need to somehow go around them.

Joey and Karen, that night they walks and carry Leo and but everywhere they when, they felt they were surrounded and then Karen said two of the snakes are near you and seems like they are going to get us.

Karen said I am not going to die here, and do you hear what I am saying Joey and we need to find out which ways out and Joey said I know. Soon it will be getting dark and we need to make a campsite but I don't think this place will be good because of the "snakes" well we have no place else and the snake will come to under the cover and we will feel them until they bite us.

"Stop freaking me out Karen and I cannot take this" but we are in the jungle and we will survivor this, just believe me and we will do well.

But am very scare and you just don't care, I do but we will make it back to the hotel and so, if you says so… I don't need your nasty remark, right now I am trying to figure out how to make it back alive to civilization, so do I said Karen.

So let work together and figure out how to get out of the jungle, fine!

Joey was putting up the tent and then Karen yelled out and said watched out I think I see cobra snake and I see an other and it red with black stripe on the back and I think it is poisonous snakes here, and I am not laying down with snake that next too me.

Looks out there is a snake on the tree and it will going to get on you come closer me now…

Karen ran toward Joey and didn't stop and ran into the jungle and Joey got up and tried too follow her, and somehow he couldn't find her.

Then Karen called out Joey and where you are and then Joey looks around Karen was near a Cheats and heard a roar and now Karen was really scare.

Joey help me just be quiet and maybe they will leave and about a minute an white tiger storm into near Karen and now Karen is being terrify and scare and was afraid too move and Joey didn't know what to do, if Leo was wake I would asked him. But Karen you will be okay, why are you saying that looks I am surround by white tiger and Cheats and snakes in the jungle.

So what else could happen to me, and Karen was really pissed about the whole safari trip and Karen said went we get out of here alive and I don't if I want to be with you Joey.

At moment the white tiger was looking at Karen and was about going toward her and Joey somehow did some disaster and the tiger follow him and Joey didn't know what will happen next.

Meanwhile Karen standing and waited for Joey too comes back but seem like for hours and hour and he didn't comes back, and she thinking how can I be here alone in the jungle and who will save me.

I don't want too died here and I do want go home and about twenty minute later, Joey came back and Karen was relief and so Karen and Joey hug and even kiss at that moment and then Karen said don't leave me again!

I won't Karen you my life and we will make it, please don't says anything right now, I won't and they both in each other arms.

Now it night and Karen and Joey sitting at the camp fire and Karen said how much of water do we have and Joey said not too much so we need to ratio the water and Karen said can have a little bit and I am very thirsty.

She got a sip of water and took some to wipe her lips and then lay her head on Joey shoulder and then she fell asleep and Joey tried to stayed wake.

Once again Joey heard a tiger roar and Joey was scare at that moment.

About five minutes Joey fell asleep and the snakes started to get closer and closer and then suddenly Karen woke up screaming and said I probably got bitten and Joey said no, then Joey said I felt something on my knee.

Joey doesn't move I think you have a snake on your knee, and I think you don't move and you will be fine and how can you say that I could end up dead.

No, yours not dying in the jungle and you will be coming home with me I just know.

They look and the snake is gone and now Karen and Joey were relief and they didn't go back to bed and it was getting lighter and lighter.

CHAPTER 9

Morning Joey and Karen and they carried Leo on the stretcher and they walks and walks for miles and miles and no sight of civilization and so Karen said Joey I am bit tired and can stop, no not right now we need keep on walking until we sees peoples around, fine. Come on we need to rest a little bit, no it will get dark soon so we need to keep on moving, okay Joey.

I feel that we are just going around circle and we are lost and we will never get out the jungle and it is your entire fault.

I didn't want to go and you make me come to here and I just wanted to stayed in the hotel and we are starving and thirsty, and I don't have the energy to move, but you must, no I am going to take a break.

Don't you understand that it will get dark and we need to find shelter and it seem, like it going to rain, but that is the less worry about, about those wild animals that could rip us apart and there will be no trace of us?

Karen I don't want to hear your whiny and you are getting me very upset and I don't want to yell at you but we need to work together and get the heck out of here, do you hear me, and Karen walk away and didn't listens what he was saying and Joey when to sees how Leo was doing but no change.

Karen walks the path and said to herself, what am I doing here?

At moment she thought that she knew how to get out of the jungle, and she called out to Joey but he didn't hear her.

Then Joey called out to Karen and she walk back and said I think I know the ways out and then we can go back home.

Are sure Karen? I am not totally positive but I think that we won't be long in the jungle and we will get back to the hotel and I will be able to take the shower.

"Well we should go now" I am still tired and so I need to rest a few minutes and so when I am ready we will leaves, but it is getting darker, and we do not have flashlights.

We will walks slowly and I will guide you with my voice and then we will reach the road out and we will be save, are you sure it won't be a dead end.

No, tonight we will be safe and not hungry and sitting in the room and watching some TV. About a minute later, they started to hear sound like lions, but they could be tigers.

I do not want to walk into the lion den or into tigers den and they will EAT US UP, it won't happen and how do you know it won't and Now Leo was getting better and stronger and he wanted to speak, because he knew the jungle but Karen decided not too listen to Leo and was like a bossy bitch.

But Joey said listen to Leo and he know his ways around here and you don't.

Thanks a lot for the insult about, and I should leave you behind with Leo, are you insane? No, but I do want to get the heck out here.

You need to know that you can fall into quicksand and you can run into wild animals that can maul you; I know that you care about me.

But we need to go now…ok let go now and so they lifted Leo on the stretcher and headed north of the mountain and Leo said your going the wrong ways and Karen started to argue with him and then he kept his mouth shut and now they were in deeper jungle than before.

Karen looks around and said let go back, and Joey said now we need to rest until morning.

But I want to go now, and Joey sat down and Karen started to walks and then looks back and Joey was not there, so she turned around and headed back.

Then she saw a cub and then the lion came toward her and she stop but didn't run and so stood there in a panic and then Karen knew it was clear she started to walk back.

Then she said where my flashlight is and I need to sees where I am going and she started to call out Joey name and then no answered.

Now Karen stop and then tears were coming down and she wanted to find Joey and Leo and she was frighten alone in the jungle.

A few steps she was getting closer to Joey and Leo and when she got back, she ran to Joey and kissed his lips and said I am sorry.

He grab her and kiss her and put her down on the ground and they kissed and hold each other tight and he felt her gentle breast and kissed her, and she kissed him back and said I will never leave you again.

CHAPTER 10

Karen got up and said, I am so, so hungry and I am thirsty too.

I know honey, they will looks for us, the search party we been out here a long time about five weeks, maybe they might will dies here in the jungle and with the wild animals and with wildcats and bats. I know and with obvious attraction are larger lions and leopard and elephants and giraffes, and zebras, so why are talking about it, you said this safari we would be safe and nothing would happen and looks, our tour is on a stretcher and we are out of foods and water, so how will we make it, so will looks for foods, and Karen said well we are going to hunt? Yes and we are going to eat and drink, and will make it back to civilization and get back home, maybe we should go back to the river and tried to go up river and it might take us back to Cape town and so we need to tried Joey and I don't want to stayed here any longer I want to leave now.

You are right we need to find peoples to get us back to "Cape Town" and we need to do it now and so if we wait it will get dark soon and we cannot travel at night on the boat and we need to be very careful with the snakes and we don't want to bitten and died from them.

So what is the plan, well we head back to the boat and carry Leo on the stretcher and we head up river, are sure going up river will take us to "Cape Town" I don't know, and Karen helped carry Leo to the boat and Joey said the river looks kind of muddied and I think we should

28

stayed here, what are you crazy? No, I just want to go home and I want to eat and drink and I am really hungry do you know how much? Yes I am starving and just get into the boat and Joey started to row and Karen said I will help you out and Leo lift his head and said go north up the river and Joey said okay I will.

So they row and row up river and there would two section of the river and Leo said take the right near the tree and it will take you to Cape town, and Karen was smiling and then she saw a snake in the boat and Karen scream out and said Joey be careful, watch you step, and it about a inch away from you and somehow Leo pull out the knife and threw it toward the snake and it was dead and Leo said well we can have snake for food, and Karen said no way.

Then Leo got up a bit and skin the snake and venom from the snake and cut it up and they ate it raw, and Karen vomit it and said I cannot eat it.

But Joey said not bad and Karen said I cannot wait to get back to the hotel and then they went up the river and then some tree got stuck on the boat and now Leo said you need to get off the boat and remove the tree, and Karen said, no Joey it is too dangerous and Joey took off his shirt and pant and jump in the water and then Karen said watched I think that I see an crocodile coming toward you and you need to get out the water and it going to eat you up and it was coming closer and closer so far Joey didn't remove the tree and Karen it freaking out and calling out to Joey, hurried come in but Joey still in the water and then Karen said I sees more crocodile coming and they are going to get you and Leo said he will be fine and about a minute later Joey got out of the water and said I am fine, Leo said well this water is infected with crocodile and snakes and we need to go now.

Karen just looks and Joey kept rowing the boat and Leo said we are headed the wrong ways, and Joey said you told me do go this ways. No sir, you did and Karen said, come on Leo tell us which ways to go back and then he somehow sat up and said empty your wallet and jewelry and Karen said I am not going to give you my diamond and Leo said well I will push Joey into the river and he going to died.

Okay I will give to you and please don't hurt us, I won't and you need to tried give me all your money and I need to leave you in the jungle so row the boat to the side, please let us go and I tell anyone and he shook his head and said no.

About ten minutes, once again Karen and Joey were in the jungle stranded and broke and hungry and thirsty, and Leo went back into the boat and row out and said, sorry I family is hungry and I needed the money and the jewelry to support my family, your just going to let us died here and how could you?

Leo left and Karen ran and shouting out and said "come back we need you too take us to the hotel" But Leo didn't even listen and headed up river and then somehow the boat started to leak and he was trying to get the water out and the he saw the crocodile coming toward him and he still had his knife and he pull it out and tried to kill the crocodile, but Leo was not strong enough and the crocodile bit off his hand and it started to bleed and then Crocodile got his leg and drag him into the water and Leo still tried too defense it but then Leo just sunk in the water and was gone.

Karen and Joey looks for shelter and Joey said I think, we can sleep here tonight and Karen said will it be okay?

Yes I think so and Karen got very close and Joey gave her a kiss and said we will get out of here and we will be fine.

CHAPTER 11

Karen and Joey lying under the stars and Joey said this is romance and Karen said, yes it is but I just don't like it in the wild and I just want to be back, we will Karen. So lay down on the ground and Joey said we will be all right and we will get back to civilization and be home and then Karen said did you sees that falling star and did you make a wish, no I miss it, but I didn't.

Then Karen got closer to Joey and hold him tight and said we need to sleep and we have a big day tomorrow and so we will be walking a lot tomorrow and Joey nodded his head and said yes we are going walks a lot.

About one minute later Karen fell asleep and Joey kept on staring at the sky and thinking, this is a romance time and Karen is sleeping in my arms.

But I will remember this night and then he fell asleep and about 4 am the rain came and it woke up Karen and Joey and they were soaked wet but in the jar was a some water and Karen said now we have something to drink and the thunder and lighting and then it stop about 7 am and Karen said well now I am not thirsty but wet. So am I Karen and the sun will dry us off.

That morning Karen and Joey got up and got ready to walks in the path of the jungle that they don't know where it might lead. But they were not giving up and they really wanted to get out jungle, but Karen was not sure if they were headed the right way out and Karen said we need to follow the sun and it will take us to the north of the jungle and will lead us to the main road.

Joey said are sure we are going into the right direction and Karen said yes and we need to follow the sun and we will be near Cape Town, where the tour started.

Little more ways and then Karen trip over a wood and feel to the ground and sprain her leg and said I cannot walks it is hurting me, but I will hold you and we will get out here and I am not going to leave you here, do hears what I am saying, yes loud and clear, but I will slow you down, don't worry about it.

Karen hold on to Joey and they walks and walks and they reach a dirt road and Joey said I don't know, what do you mean, we need to continue, and suddenly a Lions came and Karen said no, now what? I don't want to be eaten up and don't panic, I won't Joey.

About half minute and they were like following us and now what don't panic, okay I will try to relax, but every moment Karen was so frighten that she was shaking, don't show the fear to the lions and they will not hurt us, so how do you know that, I did research and so we need to very calm and we will get out here alive, okay.

But every step that they took the lions was in back of them and Joey said I don't like this but don't freak out and they will attack us.

Fine, I will just walks natural and so will you and then Joey said I sees a waterfall come up about in five minute and we can stop and looks at it.

We need to get out here and before the dark comes back and we need just keeps on moving said Karen and I don't care about the waterfall and I only care about getting the heck out here, do hear what I am saying and about ten minutes the lions when to the jungle and Joey said they left us and we are fine and Karen, right now we safe and we don't know what ahead of us, do we.

No, but I believe that we will be okay and I don't want to hear that again.

It so quiet here and I don't like that feeling that something might just jump out the jungle and eat us up and no it not going to happen, once again you are trying to insure that we will make it out the jungle, yes and we will tell our children and grandchildren about this safari, yes they will enjoy the story that we told them.

Joey we are not even married and you talking children and I am not sure that I want them, I know that you love kids so and you wanted a family, yes and that why I love you from day one.

That attract me when I first met you and you are so precious too me and I don't want to loss you, you won't.

They walks a few mile and then saw the giraffes and Joey said we are headed the right ways and so I am so happy, and Joey kissed her lips and hold her tight and then said I need to take a drink of that water but we need to ratio the water and we keep on walking I agree, said Joey to Karen.

Then they stop and it seems like it was a dead end and Karen started to cried and said, why, why did you bring me here?

I wanted us to have a romance and adventure together and so are we having adventure? Yes we are but we are also lost in the jungle and we might not even survive this adventure.

Stop this, I feel guilty about this trip and don't rub in anymore.

CHAPTER 12

They kept on walking and walking and then Karen said, why did you take us to the lion dens, and we surrounded and tried not to move fast the lions will follow us and they will jump us and we will get killed, so how do know the history about lions, well I did some research and so we need to be very careful how we move and walks and try not make yourself any attention, I won't.

Just follow my steps and don't looks at them and they won't follow us and how you know that's just trust me, I will.

They walks very slowly but the baby cub started to follow them and now what I do but don't pick it up because the lion will attack you and pull off your face.

I don't understand what you saying and I am a bit nervous about what going on right now, so don't do anything cause attention, I won't are sure you won't do I have repeat myself, no just keep on walking and don't looks at the lion.

About half hour later Karen and Joey were out the danger for an moment but then they heard some shooting and men yelling and Karen said don't let them see us, but why they can take us back to the hotel, not these men they are hunter and they are killer, so we need to hide and they cannot sees us.

Karen was frightened and Joey thought that she was only saying that about those men, but she warns Joey not to make a sound, and they were being fine.

About one hour later the hunters pass them and they waited about hour and half and then they got up and started to walks through the path and so stop for an moment but Karen said we must leave now, the hunters will be back and we need to be out of sight, and Joey said okay so we just keep going east and then west toward the sun, yes...

Once again they heard gunfire and Karen said they are very close and I don't like it and we can even get killed by them and known one would find us.

But my family knows that we came here and they would call the authority and so we are lost in the jungle, by now they contact someone to find us.

You need to believe that Karen and I would never let anyone harm you; you would have no control if they did, Joey.

Now it is not time to argue but find back to the hotel and fly home, we will get to the hotel and we will be okay.

Weeks when by and Karen and Joey still in the jungle and known is searching for them and they are on their own, and each day Karen and Joey are getting weaker and weaker and they don't have any foods or water.

Karen said we need to rest now and I don't have the energy to walks and I need to lay down and Joey said no we need to go about one more miles from here and we will be safe from the hunter and Joey said I am glad that I have this hat that you bought me and it protection from the sun.

Karen said, it was be nice to have a shower and burger and fries right now.

I am starving and Joey started to eat some berry and Karen said don't eat it can be poison and Joey swallow one and then he fell to the ground and Karen tried to wake him up and she said you better not died on me, if you do I will kill you and about ten minutes later he open his eyes and grab her and gave her a kiss and she was relief that he fine.

Then he hold her tight and said I will never let you go and Karen said we need to go now we have wasted time and it will become dark and then will have stayed.

So Joey got up and they started to walks now they got to a place, with a lot of trees and no place to camp and now Karen said, well we need to move a little more and get out this jungle.

Then Joey said I see lake, and maybe we can cross it and then but it will be dark and we stayed here until morning and then we will cross the lake, and then we might be closer to the civilization, that true and I don't want to eaten up by alligator and crocodiles, and I know what your saying and we will be fine.

So they spread out the blanket and they both got close and hold each other and then Karen said I think that I see bats around the trees and I am afraid that they might get into my hair and attack us. Now you sound paranoid and stop this.

Tonight we are under the stars and we should have a romance night, it was been if it was under different circumstance, but not now.

Come on Karen, you known that we will get back home but it just taking a little longer, I do understand but I am not in the mood now…

Then Karen just turn around and Joey was like staring at the stars and then they both fell asleep and the morning came and they had to make the decision.

CHAPTER 13

Joey is we making the right decision about crossing the lake? Yes I am sure it will take us back to village. Karen said fine and I am ready to leave this jungle and be back at home and Joey said well the bridge is not too strong so, one by one to cross, so I will go first if it is safe and so then you follow and then Karen says well if you fall into the lake and who will save you. Stop being acting like a bitch and so okay I will stop acting like this but I am tired and hungry and I want to be home and I do understand and we are going to be okay.

Joey first started to cross the bridge and the bridge was like moving and shaking and then Karen called out and said, Joey, quiet Karen I need to focus and get across and then I will help you out. I think I can do it myself. Well I want to help, fine.

Joey got across, but before he cross the bridge he thought he was going to fall down into the lakes and then he called out Karen are you ready to cross, and she nodded her head and started to walks and not fast but a slow pace and Joey was patience waited for her to come across, then there was an moment that she slip and hold on too one bridge railing and then Joey ran to her and she said are you crazy, you wanted to killed us both.

You should stayed back and now the bridge might collapse and we both will end up dead, no we won't hold my hand and then he pull her up and but also notice they had run now or end up in the lake, and so he didn't wanted to scare Karen but it was a close called.

When they both were across, Joey shown her and she said no ways we would end up being dead, if this place doesn't lead us nowhere what happened?

I don't know but we will be fine, stop saying that, I just want a bed to sleep in and not being in jungle in Africa, I hear you loud and clear.

They started to walks for miles and miles and more jungle and monkeys on the trees and Joey, joke around and said I am "Tarzan and you Jane", Karen laughed and said no more joking around, we need to get serious and we are hungry and if we don't eat we will died. Hope that we see a city that we can rest and get to "Cape town and so but we are still stuck in jungle.

We will get out the jungle and we will be home with our family again, and they must have contact someone by now. I hope that you right, Joey.

Karen said I need to stop and Joey said we need to find a place for our campsite, and Joey said not here and they walks further and further and Karen said we are being follow by someone and I am not sure, who that is? Just keep on walking and don't looks back, and when I tell you too stop, you do and we will tell them to leave us alone.

They might hurt us and you right so we need make a run for it and then we will be safe, I am ready to run and then Joey said seem like they left us and then a moment later they were in front of them with arrows and knives. And there faces were painted and they were half naked and so then they saw an lion coming toward them and one of painted tribe person came up and then they were surrounded and they didn't understand the language, one tall lady with dark skin spoke some English words, how can I help you, and Karen said we need to get back to Cape Town," the lady said you when too far into the jungle and you will have about two week to get back to civilization and you can stayed here for the night and I will give you some foods and water and you can sleep in the blue tent and where my home and you will not be harm and then she said the lion is called Leo, and it is our pet, and will not eat you and it is train.

Karen thanks the lady and she gave Karen a short shirt and gave Joey a some pants and told him that he must go to the red tent and then Karen said, I don't want to leave and I am afraid, but you will be fine.

Joey went and Karen spoke with the lady and she introduce herself to Karen said, my name is "Sun" and don't worry and then Sun lay on her blanket and Karen then lay on her and then she fell asleep and then the morning came and Karen got up and wash up and then Joey came and said this was an blessing and then Karen said we need to leave now, and she thanks Sun and Sun show them which ways out and Karen, and Joey walks and walks and it was no end.

About ten minutes later, Sun came out running said you must leave before it get dark and so just go east of this jungle and you will get to a town.

Joey and Karen walk over five mile and still no town and they felt they were walking in circle and then Karen said I sees something, and I am sure it looks like a town.

Joey stop and said this is not good I have an bad feeling that "Sun" is working with the hunters, and I think they are very near and we near go west, say if she was telling the truth and then we end up in the jungle again, we should tried Sun was she was saying, are going take the risk of our lives.

CHAPTER 14

Yes we are risking our lives but I am willing to find out if we will get out this jungle and that all Joey, but if she is a liar we will never get out, someone much be looking for us, I know you said that before but, I am praying to god that they are. Come on and think with me and maybe we will get out the jungle and so, well we will not do it tonight and where we are headed seem like we will be worst off and so we need to find peoples and show us the ways out.

I know what you saying but the sun is going down and it will be dark soon and we need to make the camp here and in the morning we will figure out how to get out of here, in the first place if we when to Hawaii instead we would not be stranded in the jungle, and wild animals running around and so I don't want to argue with you.

I feel that we are being watched and I don't know but now you are sounded like you paranoid but you are right we are not alone.

So should be do? Nothing but don't let them know that we know that they are looking and watching and it might be the hunters and I don't want to be hunter by them, I know I don't neither.

Then Joey came up to Karen and gave her a big kiss and so why did you do that Joey, well they watching us so I just make it looks that we don't know what happening around us.

Good idea and I hope that they leave and we can be quiet and then Joey said I probably will tried to go to them and get some foods and waters and Karen said are you crazy and don't leave me and I am scare and so Joey hold her tight and said I won't let you go, and she smiled and said good.

Joey lit the fire and they sat there and hold hands and kiss and she said it is a "Moon full" and he looks up and said yes it is and it is a night to remember.

Then they lay near the fire and then Karen scream and said I saw an snake move on the ground and it looks red with brown skin and it make a sound and Joey said well I can kill it and we can eat it and I will squeeze the venom out the snake and Karen said be careful.

It is a poisonous snake around here and I am so afraid that we will die in the jungle and they will found bones.

About half hour later, Karen fell asleep in Joey arms and Joey was not sleeping because he was doing watched and he was afraid that they might be in danger.

It was about 4 am and Joey somehow fell asleep and then he heard a sound and it was an lion standing over his head and Joey didn't move and he just kept quiet and then the lion just left and Joey was relief and about two hour later, Karen got up and said so did anything happen and Joey with a smile and said no everything is okay, and Karen said I am ready to leave this place and so am I said Joey.

So they pick some stuff and Joey said I am so hot and I just want to take off my shirt and Karen said I should change into my short and tee shirt and so where is out stuff, don't tell me that we lost our stuff and most of all our money and passport and how are we going to get back home? Joey will don't worry I will contact our folk and so we will be fine and then they walks about five miles and now they are out of the jungle.

But now the situation got worst, they ended up in the deserts and the sand all around and it was really hot and Karen said we should go back to the jungle.

No, we will go through the desert and then we will get to the road and then we will be back to cape town and then we be near the hotel, you think so said Karen, we will died in the deserts for sure., no we will not said Joey.

The sun was burning there skin and Karen was like losing her balance and Joey was trying to help her and then they stop and Joey said I see water and I will run and get some and Karen just fell to the ground and Joey ran to imagination in his mind and no water and then he got back and said Karen wake up and but she was out cold.

Joey looks around and thought which ways we go and then he carry Karen in his arms and then he thought he saw a house and then he carry Karen and then stop and he fell himself.

Karen woke up and thought she saw a black man with a hat standing above and said, please mister, help us….

Karen was dreaming and Joey got up and said Karen, we need to move now, it will be cold at night we need to walks a little more and out of the desert.

Karen agrees and said yes we do and let do it and Joey said are you okay? Yes don't worry about it and then they walks a mile and they stops.

CHAPTER 15

They looks around and Karen said we should have stayed in the jungle and known one will found us now, we are doom in the deserts and I don't like this at all stop whinny, you have been complaining from day one when we arrival to Africa, that is not true, Joey, yes it is Karen. Joey got up and he started to walks and he thought he saw water but it was only a mirage and Joey just sat down near the tree and Karen wanted to call out and said there is a snake coming closer to you, and he said what? Then Joey saw the snake and took out the knife and stab the snake and it was about an inch away from him.

Then Joey when back to Karen and said we will eat raw snake but I squeeze the venom and we will have a meal and Karen was not too happy but had no choice.

So Joey cut up the snake in ratio into pieces and Joey said we cannot eat the whole piece but eat slowly, I will, and Joey looks at Karen and she was suntan and fragile and with the hat on and with blue short and bugs crawling on her leg and Karen tried to killed them and Joey said be careful they might be harmful, I know said Karen to Joey.

Joey got up and said that we have about 10 miles to the road and Karen said I cannot make it, we will make it and we will be fine...

Karen got up after she ate the piece of the snake and Karen said it is time to go now it is daylight and it get really dark early here. So we should walks about miles and two, and Joey said are you sure? Yes I am and so they both started to walks and Karen stop for a moment for rest and then they continue and Joey said I see something ahead and Karen said it might be a mirage and don't says that. I won't and so Joey walks a little quicker and then he stop and waited for Karen to get closer and Joey said I am exhaust and I need to rest and Karen said just for five minutes and then we keep on going until we reach the end of this desert, okay I agree…

The sun was going down and it begin to get dark and Joey said tonight we will have camp here and tomorrow we will go further and Karen agree and then they set up the tent and Karen got closer to Joey and she was shiver and he hold her tight and they kiss and had to body together to keep warm.

Joey wanted to speak but Karen just kissed his lips and that night they make hot passion love and Joey was on top of her and kiss her all over and brace is hand on her breast and squeeze and suck it, and Karen was getting excited and then they heard noises and Joey and Karen listen and they were not sure what they would hearing but it sounded like water sound.

Joey got up and left Karen and Karen called out and said where are you going and Joey said over there I sees some water, wait for me.

Karen got up and Joey came back and they put the tent and carry it and it was the river and Karen said now we are out of the desert, yes we are. Now Karen started to eat twigs and even tried to eat little bugs and Joey said what are you doing? Trying to stay alive. Then Joey started to eat bugs that he could catch and eating the twigs and Joey and Karen after they ate they relax in each other arms and kissed one more time., then the rain came and Joey had container to keep the water and so they had some water and it kept them going.

When the rain stop and it started to be very hot and humid and Karen said I need to take off my top and keep my bra on and I will feel a little cooler and Joey remove his pant and sat in his underpants and Joey looks up and said it will be a hot one day, and Karen shook her head and then she saw a snake coming toward them and it was really big and

Karen was about to scream but Joey cover her mouth and he stab the snake and but almost got bitten at that time. Once again Joey squeeze the venom out of the snake and then they skin off and ate it raw and now Joey and Karen were getting a bit stronger and drank some water and lay down and look up the sky.

Karen started to speak but Joey was fast asleep and then she cuddles next him and put her head on his chest.

The sun was beaming hot and it was like torch and but when the night came., it was really cold, and Joey got up and pull up his slack and then put on his shoes and walk away for a minute and looks around and put up the tent and then carry Karen inside and make passion love.

About one hour later they heard a roar and Karen said what is out in front of our tent and he peek out it was an "white tiger" and his mouth was open wide and was about to attack and then they heard gunshot and Karen and Joey kept quiet and make sure, known one would see them.

So the tiger escape with no harm and so Karen and Joey stayed inside and waited until the gunshots were gone.

At that moment Joey said to Karen it is time for us to leave this place and I think there are a lot of bad peoples around here so we need to very quiet and walk very fast and Karen said I got it.

CHAPTER 16

Karen and Joey pick up the stuff they had and headed out of the desert and they reach the river and now they needed to found a boat to sail out from there.

So are going to build a boat and with woods and tie with twigs and then they sail away and get home, and it will take times. But we will be here for while and it will be much better, then being in desert and now near from the lake.

I feel safer than the jungle but we still in the jungle and but the peoples, might come and rescue, do think so. Yes maybe someone will see...

We need to figure how to get out of jungle and be in the warm bed, and taking a shower, and having cook foods and not eating raw snakes, and bugs and some kind of grass, and then Joey said I am not feeling that great and he was shaking and shriving and couldn't stand and so sat down and Karen felt his head and it was hot and she said, so you don't died on me.

About a minute later, Joey fell asleep on the ground and Karen was like in tears and was about to cried and then she saw a cheetah in the tree and then Karen looks up and the cheetah jump on the second tree and Karen wanted to follow but then she changed her mind and stop and looks at Joey.

Karen got some firewood and lit the fire and looks around and then a wild cat came toward the camp and Karen had no weapon to defense from the wild cat and Karen didn't panic, but move slowly and wild cat, stolen the fish and left and now Karen thought what she was going to eat and but she didn't want to leave Joey alone because he might be attack.

There were baobab plants, trees near the lakes and Karen kept on looking for someone to come and rescue them but no one came to save them.

Joey was laying there and toss and turning and Karen check his forehead and he still had a little fever and Karen wet his lips with water and then he woke up and wanted to get up but he was too weak to walks and so Karen told him too lie down and he did and then he fell asleep and Karen watched guard and so Karen didn't sleep all night and so the next morning Karen when near the lakes and caught a fish but then she was surround a by an snake, with red stripe and very fatal, so she tried to move slowly and not get bitten.

Joey got up and went toward her and said, don't worry and he kill the snake and she asked how you doing and he are said I am doing much better.

Then he grabs her hand and said we will stay here for a while and then we will move up the lakes and we will be better off.

Karen said well this place is good and why can we stayed here, Well we might run into more snakes and wild cats. I know about that's and Joey said let move on and Karen said are going to build a boat to sail out of here? Not today but maybe tomorrow when I am much stronger, fine.

I thought we would be home by now but we are still stuck in Africa and so I don't like it, do you understand what I am saying to you, Joey said stop complaining and maybe tomorrow we will be back at the hotel.

I would to be home right now and not in the jungle and I don't like this adventure, well we never had to learn how to survive and now we do and we miss our Mr. Coffee and our shower and material stuff that we have, yes that true. Yes I miss that thing and I am human and so am I said Joey...

About a minute later Joey walks way and Karen said don't leave me, I need to looks around and found a ways out and then we can use the path out and so yes that is an good ideas, and so looks around and don't go too far and don't leave me and he said "silly girl".

Stop calling me silly girl, well we need to joke around and then Karen said find us the ways out now, I am I will, I promise…

About two hour later, it feel like it going to rain and Joey said well I will not take that little walk but tomorrow morning I will. Sure you will.

I don't need you too be rude to me and so and acting like a bitch, no I am not acting like a bitch.

Karen didn't speak to Joey and Joey just went into the tent and left Karen out near the fire and Karen walk in and he was snoring away and Karen just went inside the cover and when to sleep and the next morning when Karen woke up Joey was gone and she called him out and nothing and now she was afraid that she is alone…

About five hour later Joey, was walking around and he was not sure what direction to walks back and so Karen was really worry but she couldn't do anything and so Karen just waited and waited for Joey to comes back.

But Joey didn't comes back that night and Karen was scare and frighten and noises in the jungle, and just went into the tent but didn't check for snakes.

CHAPTER 17

Karen zipped up the tent and she heard a roars and then she looks out and she was surrounded by "White Tigers" and they rip up the bags and stole the fishes that she caught and she took the raw snake and now Karen was very quiet and scare to come out, and then she heard footsteps and she peek out of the tent and didn't wants anyone too see her. But the tiger smell her and want to rip the tent and get inside and Karen was moving on the other side and the tiger follow her and Karen was terrify at that moment and she didn't know if Joey was dead or alive and Karen, didn't have a weapon to shoot the tiger and the tiger was roaring and putting his paws inside and trying to claws and Karen just move around the tent and then it got rip torn and tiger was inside and about a minute later, there was a shot and the tiger was laying on the ground and she saw a men with guns and now think that they will take her way and she will never know what happen to Joey, but meanwhile Joey was walking and walking in the jungle and then he figure out to get back to the camp, and meanwhile Karen sat on the ground and one of the we have the tiger and now we should leave but the other hunter wanted to take Karen and so she wouldn't tell the authority about the tiger kill and they said miss you will not tell anyone that we tell this white tiger and she shook her head and said no, just go and they pick up the tiger and one of the hunter wanted to knife her and he pointed

49

the knife toward her face and said, if you says anything we will be back and we will kill you miss.

So Karen said don't worry I promise I won't tell a soul and I do keep my word.

Later that day, somehow Joey got back to camp and saw the blood and he ran in and said are you okay, Karen? Then Karen said where have you been and I could have been killed and you were somewhere in the jungle.

Joey then spoke and said no, I didn't found a way out from here and we need someone to found us. Karen said well it will be a long time, I hope not.

Then they cuddled and Joey said to Karen I love you and she said "thank you" and Joey said well your welcome and then said I thought you love me too, I do Joey but things are not good and we are stranded in the jungle of Africa and no one is searching for us.

They could be looking, but not in this area, well we will have got ourselves out and then we will make it out.

Joey said to Karen I will go north and south. Your not going alone I am going with you too, do you understand, we will be doing things together and I don't to sit at the campsite and I could have been attack by tiger and hunters could comes so, Joey I am coming along and I could keep up and we can think of plan how to get out of here, yes your right, so tell me the truth, would threaten by anyone when I left you alone, no but I am just telling you, I do not be left alone in the jungle, and then Joey gave her a kiss and then they heard sound of footsteps in the jungle and they would loud boom and Joey said it sound like a stamped of elephants coming through and it is an pack and we need to move now, I got it Joey.

About ten minutes the elephants were in the camp and they were going toward the lakes to drink the water and Karen do not let sees us, and there were little elephants and largest elephants coming toward them and it was really terrify time and Joey and Karen ran and ran and ran go quick and then they stop at the end and then Karen saw an snakes crawling up the tree and Karen said we cannot stand here and if we do the snake will bite us.

A way up there would surrounded by leopards and Karen said we were better off with elephants and Joey said you would right should stayed, why did we move who will save us now. Don't make any crazy move, they attack, and we will end being there meal.

Joey hold I am scare and I don't want to died and just stand still and don't move, then she was about to scream, because snakes were coming toward them and they couldn't run because the leopard were going attack but they had to make an life and death decision in second and Karen and Joey ran and the leopard follow them and Joey said don't let back, just keep on running and then Joey said don't hear an helicopter, I do but how do we get their attention we don't. What do mean we don't?

They could be the bad hunters and they could killed us and we will died, so they might help us and get out of here and you are willing to take a chance with our lives?

Yes if we got out the jungle and we got back to civilization, I would risk it.

But I wouldn't because they could feed us to the leopards and we would be heard again, Joey you really scaring me and I don't like it at all.

So keep on moving and we will be fine, and we will ourselves to get out of here and we don't need anyone but ourselves and I think that you stupid.

CHAPTER 18

Karen stop calling me names and we need to walk this path and I think it will lead us to the river and the lakes we will leave and we will be fine, if you says so, and Karen kept on walking and then said my feet are hurting me and Joey said just walk and shut up your whiner and Karen said I know how you are and you mean too mean since this adventure and I don't like your attitude, well should say what I don't like about you, you are afraid of new things and I do want to have more adventure and sees things, and you don't understand me and sometime yours not on the same pages, well that how you feel about me and now I sees how you are and I don't like you but I love, about us being together and I am sure when we get out the jungle out alive, I will think about it. Yes what is the plan, well I will build a hut and we will have shelter and we will have a roof over our head, I didn't want that answered, I wanted the answer to be went we were leave this place, I don't but I will try to build a draft and then we can float on the river to get to our destiny and then we will be back home and Karen said really no one is searching for us, I think they think that we died, no that not it and I think we just when off a bit way and they don't know the location, I guess so.

Joey said I guess I better start building but I don't have the proper tools, but somehow I will manage with the twigs and vines and we will have some shelter if it rain, Karen started to help Joey with carry the vines and twigs and then Karen hand it over to him and then hold a vine and the twigs.

Then Joey said I need to take a break and my arms are sore and so are mine said Karen to Joey and they both sat down, and then they heard someone, and sound and she said it could be someone looking for us and Joey said we are in dangerous land and we need to be careful. What do you mean?

Well, when I mention dangerous peoples, just like the hunters, yes I know but they are not around, so how do you know if they really left, I don't but I hope so, and then Joey said I heard someone is lurking and I don't like it.

They will attack us and maybe even killed us and now Joey you are scaring the crap out of me.

Later that night Joey was looking out and Karen was fast asleep and didn't hears any commotion, and Joey was almost attack but he fight back and it was an wild cat that wanted to bite him so Joey hit him over the head and it fell and move the wild cat and went back to the camp, but now he knew that he been watched and he was sure who was there!

The next morning he woke up Karen and said we need to leave this campsite and Karen said why? I think the hunters are here, are sure?

No, but someone was lurking at us from the bushes and I also had to killed and wild cat. So a lot things went down when I was sleeping and that is right, said Karen to Joey, so why we just go and I will pack our stuff and we will head out of here, and about a minute later, Joey said the "hunter are back".

Karen picks her stuff and Joey things and has soon they started to walk, they saw the hunter behind them and Joey said we need to walk faster and faster and Karen said slow down you are walking too fast for me...

The hunters were about half mile behind them and then they started to shoot at them and Joey said duck down and Joey did the same and Joey said we will not get shot and Karen said how do you know that we won't get shot?

Just stayed low and make sure that they don't see us.

Okay, Joey but we cannot be a target for them and we need to get way from here, yes I know…

They stop for a moment and they stand for a second and then the hunters were pointed the gun at them and Joey was saying please don't kill me and the one of the hunter said I want your woman, and she said never you will not have me.

Joey boy, you give us your lady friend and we will let you go and Joey said I am leaving Karen and you are not going to have her, and Karen was screaming loud and one of the hunter, hey lady no one will save you.

Then Karen said tell me your name, and he said my Ben and my friend is Rex and you are one hot lady here and we want to have fun with you and your friend is no match of lover has we are.

I do not want you Ben or Rex, let us go and I will tell anyone, and Ben said I am going to have and no one will stop it, you will force to have sex with you what kind of men are you savage?

No, we are the really men that you will have the pleasure and really passion and not like your friend the geek

No he is not a geek, he is my fiancé and I love him and then they push Joey on the ground and said watched what we are doing.

CHAPTER 19

Somehow Joey mange to get up and grab their guns and pointed at them and at the time Ben was holding Karen and at that time Ben said drop the gun and your girlfriend won't get hurt, but Karen said don't listen to him shoot him and I will be fine, Karen then bite him and got loose and Joey and Karen somehow had rope and tied them up and Karen said they have a phone and I can called someone and Ben said, you will reach more of my friends and they will comes and cut you up you cant and Joey went up to him and whack his face and even some blood bleed from his face and Ben said I will fix you when I untied myself and Joey left go we have some kind ways to get out the jungle with there jeep, then Ben said you will not get too far, do you get it.

We will get far ways from you and we will tell the authority what you did and try to rape my fiancée and you will go to jail, and Ben and Rex we have friends and we will not go to jail, but when we catch up to you, you will be sorry.

Don't threaten me, you're tied up and you will get untied and you will not find us and we will and we will killed you and your lady friend and will make sure you see her when we killed her in front of your eyes. Don't listen to him, Karen we will be fine and we will make sure that they won't hurt anyone else again.

So they left them tied up and got into the jeep and drove off and Karen said there is not enough fuel to get far, I will tried to get us out of the jungle and into the main stream and then we contact the authority and so that is the plan said Joey to Karen and don't worry about anything at all. We are safe from Ben and Rex, but we are still in the jungle and we are not safe from the wild life, that is true, but now have a jeep and we will find civilization.

Check their bags for foods and water and then we will not be so hungry and thirsty, I will check and she open the one of the bags and threw it out of the jeep and what was it? Skins of an animals and so bloody, and so she open the second one and it was more skins and she threw it out and said I guess we will starve a little longer, and check for water and nothing.

Then he stops for a moment and said; now we need to walk the rest of the ways we are out gas. So they got out the white jeep and started to walk and then suddenly Joey fell into quicksand and Karen said I will get some vine and pull you out and Joey said hurried up, I am sinking too fast, I am.

About a minute later, Karen was pulling out Joey out quicksand and she was really pulling and pulling and he was safe out and then they heard a roar. Sound and it was coming toward then and it was not alone and it was about five white tigers and they were coming really close, that one of the white tiger put the claw on Joey chest, and some blood fell to the ground and Joey said I am okay and Karen was like freaking out and trying not to panic and so then one the tiger try to push Karen to the ground and Karen just move slowly away and Joey was still trap and bleeding from his shoulder.

Karen is careful move slow and don't looks at them in the eye, and Karen said I won't but I will not let you be here alone and I am leaving you behind.

You must, or we both will died, no I am going and I am staying and I am going to save you, don't be a stupid bitch and looks for help and I will be okay. How can you go the tiger is on you and you are bleeding? I will be fine. Stop calling me a bitch and I am going to save you, and

Joey said we both will died if you are so bad and you don't want to listen to me, no I am staying.

About a minute later the two white tigers were coming closer to Karen and Joey said you make the situation worst by staying and I told you too go and you don't, I don't like being boss around by anyone but I was trying to save your life.

Well, I am a bit stubborn and so I cannot help and so I just to be with you in any circumstance even in danger. And we don't know if Ben and Rex got loose and they can be on our trail too.

That true, but now we are in really bad danger, and they will eat us up and rip us a part into pieces.

No, we will survive this too, and don't looks into the tigers eyes and just walk slowly toward me and Joey said I can because I hurt my knee, and I am in pain.

Try to crawl too and don't give up, and don't let the tiger sees you, I won't dear.

When you called me dear, I know that we are in big, big trouble and we need to find the way out, yes I agree. Once again the tiger somehow roar at Joey and then he put his claws on him and Karen thought he were a goner, then some shot were fired and the tigers were laying on the ground and Joey and Karen said now we need to go and I think, Ben and Rex are back but I am sure.

So Karen picks up the stuff and Joey took a stick and they headed out and someone shouts out and said you are going deeper in the wilderness.

CHAPTER 20

Karen said maybe we should listen to those men and they might show us the ways back to the hotel, or to the tour guide station.

No, we will keep on walking and we will find the ways out ourselves.

At that time Karen didn't really wants go into the jungle and just want to go around the river and Joey, was saying no, we need to go this ways.

The sun was beaming and Karen was sweating and Joey barely could walks, and like ten minute later, they saw helicopter, yelling out and saying, are Joey and Karen, and she was about to called out and Joey said it could be them.

At that point they ran into the bush and Joey and Karen hid for an hour and came out and the helicopter was gone. But Joey does remember the first day of the safari? Yes I do but why? Remember the day that we got into that jeep and headed to the safari, yes and the first stop, yes but tell me, okay I will.

First we when for breakfast and then we when into the jeep and we went to see the "Lions and the cubs and so the Leo said it was the Pride of lions.

Then we when to Lobo hill and we saw the sleeping lions around the Lama triangle, yes I know.

So go on, then we saw an leopard in an acacia tree, and I was scare that it might jump out of the tree, okay, so you are saying you frighten and scare and you are afraid that it might attack us and but I been attack and but it known that you are here too, I know but it is too late and I cannot leave and it will follow me, you right and it will follow you attack you so hope that someone will rescue us, or we will be dead meat.

Remember the Elephants at the SILALE swamp, yes I do and I don't want to talk about the safari right now when we are in the jungle and being watched by the white tiger, fine. I won't say anything.

About the beautiful giraffes near the bank of MARA river and that was in North Serengeti and your right, and now we have survive without guide that stole our money and passport left in the jungle to died.

Karen said we will get out of the jungle and report him to the authority and he probably long gone and spending our money. Karen said we are alive and we will get out here and we are also being hunter by Rex and Ben.

I don't think we are being hunter by this tiger that won't let us leave; we need some kind of diversion and so who will do the diversion and run for help? Joey said I will distract the tiger and you run for your life, and you will listen what I tell you, fine I will and so Joey somehow threw a stick and then Joey started to run and then the tiger follow him but Karen was a little slow and then Karen ran and looks a back and was looking for Joey and but she didn't see him but she kept on running and running and she got to the river and saw some peoples and calling out and I need your helped but they didn't hear her.

Meanwhile Joey was running and he ran into an cheetah and now he was surround by an white tiger and cheetah and now he knew he had an problem and so he knew that he couldn't make an sound and about ten minutes he worst enemy came and said "I told that I will sees again" and it no lies and then he pointed the gun and Joey thought he was going to shoot him but he aim the gun toward the tiger and shot the gun and the tiger lay on the ground and the cheetah got shot and Rex came and said where your lady? Not here and left, so you are going take us where she is? You owe us your life so the reward you will give us is Karen, do you understand and he was pointed the gun at him and told him to walk and not to do anything stupid.

Ben said I know how to be in the bush and you don't and I will take you to your hotel but first need to be with your lady friend, Joey said why?

I just want her and you don't know how to treat that kind of lady and so I want to be with her and then Rex said we will show her a good time with a real men.

But she is far gone and you will not find her, well she will comes back and she is afraid to be alone so she will looks for you, so how do you that's I just know.

Karen decided to follow the river and then she stops and thought about Joey but just kept on walking and Joey said to Ben and Rex, she just kept on going and she didn't like the jungle and she will get help and the authority will comes and find me and they probably will arrest you too.

No, they need to catch us so Karen was looking and behind and if Joey was near but she just once in while looks back, and then stop and had a sip of water and she knew that she was not too where the safari started.

Joey was in front of Ben and Rex and they were holding a gun and then said if you make wrong turn, I will shoot you in the back and I think I know where your girlfriend is going and she will cause trouble, no you guys did.

CHAPTER 21

Karen then stop and looking and then sat down and was exhaust and was thinking of Joey her boyfriend and she thought maybe should head back but one thing that she remember that Joey told her to keep going and found help and rescue him from the tiger and about twenty minutes later Karen got up and started to walks and then she saw the monkeys in the trees and one of the monkey jump on her shoulder and Karen didn't know what to do.

Ben, Rex, Joey, stop at near the path and Ben said, tonight this will be our camp and Joey don't do anything stupid I will shoot you, I know you will.

About five minutes later Rex got up and when into the jungle with a lot tree and said I need to pee so, Ben said just watched where your going and Rex said I know the jungle and I will be fine, so he walks up the ways and he was going to pee, and took the left and walks the ways and stop and those it was clear and about five minutes later and Ben heard Rex screaming and so the white tiger jump him in the bush and Ben wanted to help him and about two minute later, they saw the tiger drag him and he was bleeding and he was torn and rip from the inside out and it was a bad thing to see, and Joey said well your friend got killed, yes it is a bit risking in the bush and the jungle of Africa.

Karen got up and said now I need to move but it was getting dark and she needed to use the flashlight so she decided to stayed there and start a fire. Sat quietly and thought about her boyfriend and wish that he was with her.

Karen didn't want to be alone, and she was afraid that she might get attack by a wild cat and known one would find her.

Ben said to Joey now you will be my partner and so you will make a lot of money and you will become a hunter and Joey said no thanks and Ben was pointed a gun toward Joey and you will do what I tell you don't understand, I don't want no part of killing animals.

Fine, I will show you the ways out and you will be back with your girlfriend if she make it alive, what do you mean? Well my friend got killed by a tiger and we don't know if Karen is alive, that is true but I know that she is a survivor.

I guess you believe what you want to believe and so Joey said, can we talk about something else, okay we can, and then Joey said "watch out" there is an snake coming toward you, and Ben pull out his knife and killed it and it was about an inch away and Ben said you save your enemy and so you're a bad friend, so don't called me your friend, I am not, okay.

Snakes and snakes, and they were surrounded and they were red stripe and brown and it was a poisonous snake coming toward both of them and Joey said, I will stand up slowly and then you stab them and we will remove the venom and skins and then we will have raw snake for foods.

Meanwhile Karen sat and looks around and up at the stars and moon, but Karen was under the bats and wild cats, and Karen thought it was okay but she didn't have anything to defense herself, and now she was getting worry if she was going to end of dead in jungle and surrounded by the wild and the wildness around and didn't sees any road yet. No, am I going the right ways and so is Joey fine, and now she panic and scare of her life.

Then the thunder and lightings and rain were pouring hard and so Karen decided to go into the cave and stayed warm and not to get wet.

It was pitch black and her flashlight was dim and Karen was afraid of the dark and she had long Jean torn on her knees and you can see the dirt and the cuts on her knees, and so she walk inside and looked around and waited until the rain stop and wanted to wait until morning and she had some fire woods and started a fire and kept her warm.

But Karen couldn't leave her eyes open and her hair was going into her eyes and she move it with her hand and then thought if I had an mirror I would sees how I looks, and so she fell asleep and the next morning she got up and wipe herself off and then took her stuff from the cave and started to walks up hill to the road and one old red truck with children and ladies and men in back and she yelled out and so they stop and pick her up and took her to town and she started to speak what happen on the safari, and they said we will take you to the authority and they will help you out and so they drove through the dirt road and then they stop when the tiger jump out and Karen said, oh no!!

The tiger jump toward the truck and Karen said it going to eat us up and they said don't worry we will be fine, and then she looks at the tiger eyes and she said your right and but more tigers came and now they surrounded the truck and they started to "roars" and Karen wanted to jump off the truck and one of the men hold her and told her not to looks at their and so she listens and then about ten minutes the tigers left the road and they started up the truck and headed to town, and now Karen was relief that she was going to North Serengeti, and she asked is far from Cape town and one men said shook his head and said yes, and that where my hotel is, and they looks at Karen with her long blonde hair and with the blue eyes and slim and about 5 feet and 6 inch tall and but she was a bit worry, about the men and ladies, and children.

CHAPTER 22

They drove Karen to the authority and Karen thanks them and asked if they can take her to "Cape Town and they said sorry miss we cannot we are going to the Cape Town, we are going to sees the doctor at the village.

So Karen thanks them and she walk into the police station and told them what happen, on the safari and told the police man that they were rob my the tour guide and he took the passport and the money and my boyfriend Joey still in the jungle and might be hurt and the policeman said tell me where he is and we will found him, we will use helicopter and we will find him if he is alive.

We will take you to the hotel and you will waited for your boyfriend there, and Karen said I want to go along with you and the policeman said it is really dangerous out there and you cannot go, so they walk her into the jeep and a lady drove her to "Cape town" and drop her off at the hotel and then Karen said wait a minute and said what happen if my room is gone, don't worry, I explains to them what happen to you, so she step out and walks inside with Karen and the desk clerk, said where have you been? Then Karen said we were in the jungle over the month, and we were lost and somehow we survive, so where is your boyfriend, the police are searching for him right now.

About half hour later Karen was taking a shower and washing her hair and then she got out the shower and wipe herself off and got dress into her p j, and sat on the bed and drank some water and eat some fruits. Then Karen lay in bed and was thinking of Joey and wandering if she will sees him again and thought why did I leave him in the jungle and think he need me, what do I do?

Karen got up and thought, well I cannot just sit and wait for Joey to comes back I need to hire someone to take me back into the jungle to search for the man that I love, and I pray to god that he is not hurt.

So what do I do? Karen picks up the phone and called the desk and said I want to rent a helicopter to fly over North Serengeti, and search for Joey.

When she spoke with that person, she will pay a lot of money to find her fiancé and want him to be fine.

But known one would accept her offer so she thought to hire someone to take her for an safari, and so Roy was around and she said take me to the same places that Leo took us, and he said fine, so what happen to Leo, and said he took our money and I don't know. That is not true Miss.

Leo would never steal, he was an honest man and she had a family.

So you don't believe but it did happen and so Joey and I were in the jungle and we had no foods and water and he got bitten by an poison snake but he suck out the venom, and Joey and I when through a lot and I make back and I need to found Joey, and would you help me? Yes miss, but don't accuse my friend Leo.

I don't know what happen to Leo, but he did steal my diamond ring, and our money. Then Roy said we will leave in the morning at dawn, and she said fine.

That night Karen couldn't sleep and so she stayed up and thought about Joey and she needed to find him, and she didn't listen to the police to stay in the hotel and she was anxiety and worry about the man of her love, and he meant a lot to her.

That night Karen called her family and told them that she is going on the safari and didn't tell them that she was going to search for Joey and to Joey family told them that they are having a good times and his sister wanted to speak to Joey and Karen said he was taking a shower.

Then she hung up the phone and when to bed, and she was started to have nightmare that Joey was laying in pile of blood.

So Karen woke up and walks around the room and then check if the door was closed and then when back to sleep and about 5 am, Roy knock at the door and she said I will be ready in ten minutes and she got dress and went with Roy, step out of the hotel and got into the jeep and he drove way and she said where are we headed and he said the first safari stop and she said that fine.

About two hours later they were in the wilderness and Karen said we are really in the deep of jungle, have you request and Karen said yes and you will not leave me, yes I won't miss.

You can called me Karen, and so they drive through and then he stop and now we have too walk and she said okay, so do you have an walking talking with you to communication in case that we need help, and he said yes Karen I do.

Karen was relieved and she just wanders where Joey is?

But no sign of him and she was a bit worry and then she said, it going to get dark soon, so are going to stayed here?

But Roy said no not here and about a mile away from here, and she said ok.

CHAPTER 23

They walks a mile and then he put up two tent and he had an rifle in his hand and said, you take the blue tent and I stayed and keep watched and Karen said okay, and about 45 minutes Karen woke up because she heard a gun shots and got up in the hurried and saw Roy face down and she scream and no one heard her and now Karen is on her own and then she saw Ben and Joey walking toward her and Ben said I knew you would come back, and Karen said why did you kill him, and Ben said I don't have explains anything too you, and Joey what matter with you? I am fine and Ben is a friend, since when?

When he save me from the tiger and you left me and she said you told me to leave, well I thought you would get help but you just went, but I came back for you with Roy and why did Ben killed him, well Roy stole and then killed his friends, and you believe his story, I do. Are you really telling the truth about Roy and Leo and Ben said yes he killed my best friend and left him dead in the jungle and I been searching for him for five years so he bought him and I really appreciate your help, so I show the way out and you will be safe once again, Joey will go home with you and Joey said I like being in the jungle.

But you need to know it is very dangerous out here and any wild animal might attack you, I think that you should just go with Karen, and then they all walk and walks for miles and then they stop and Ben said, I need to rest and then suddenly a tiger jump out on Ben and drag him away and Karen said what going to happen too us? We will get out here, just believe I will.

One hour later seem like they were walking around in circle and Joey Said I need to rest for a moment, and Karen said not too long, we are being followed by a vicious tiger, yes I know, about a minute later they walk again.

Karen said I am thirsty and really hungry and I want to eat something, but they saw poison fruit but Joey said don't pick it and Karen said I know.

Then they sat down and resting for hours and hours and then the night came and Karen said we need to start a fire and set up the tent and Joey said yes we do, and about half hour later, they were in the tent and it was close and the camp fire was burning and Karen said I thought I would see you again, that why I when looking for you and so Joey said you were safe and you could been home and Karen said not without you, Joey. Then they kissed and Joey said now we sleep and we will get up early and found our ways out of the jungle and I promise that too you, my love.

So Karen kissed him back and said "I love you too" and fell asleep in his arms.

The next morning Joey and Karen have to figure out how to get out of the jungle and not getting attack by the tiger and drag into the jungle and being chews up But Joey was about a bit skeptic and also worry that they might dies in the jungle and it all his fault. But Karen was still sleeping and Joey was picking up the stuff that they have but the foods was missing and Joey knew that the tiger came back and stole the foods from them.

Then Karen got up and said what wrong Joey? Joey said everything is fine, and tell me the truth, Joey, it is not fine and we do have a problem and without Ben we are stuck in the jungle, something like that's!

Karen said well it is daylight and so we should started walking and Joey said okay and they have more than five miles too go and they don't where the road might lead, so Karen just kept quiet and Joey was silent and worry.

They reach the other side of the river and Karen said I think that we need to be careful of the quicksand, yes and we are not strong enough to help each other so you are warning you and me too

Okay, Karen spoke and said I am tired and I just want to rest and we have time to rest and Joey said no it get really dark in the jungle.

Fine, but my feet hurt and I cannot walks so much miles and Joey said don't want to get out the jungle? Of course I do.

One hour later Joey said so this will be our campsite tonight and Karen said it looks like an good spot so okay, so I will lit the fire and I watched guard tonight, and Karen when into the tent and went to sleep.

Joey sat near the fire and his eyes were closing and Karen was in the sleeping bag and Karen didn't hear any sound of the jungle and Joey was fast a sleep and when Karen got up Joey was really near the fire and Karen called out and said, is trying to burn you? He nodded his head and said no, but you almost did, you don't say!

Later that day, they pack there stuff and headed out of the part of the jungle and they reach a path and Joey said do we take it? Karen said why not.

I think that we are going the right way, and Joey said how you know, I just have a feeling.

It does not make us safe but it might be the right route out?

CHAPTER 24

Karen said, to Joey, are we going the right way out and Joey said I think so and Karen was a bit worry and Joey was just off track and confuse and seem like they walks at the same place for three times and Karen said we have been here and what wrong with you Joey? Nothing wrong with me, seem like it is and he wanted to argue, but Joey said not now...

Let me think, and then Joey said do you have your compass, I am not sure but I will check.

Karen looks and said nope I don't have it, so where is yours? I might have lost it when I was with Ben, okay so I lost mine when I was on my own and I don't know...

Then there was a sound they heard and Joey said the predator is following us and we need to walk slow and not run, if we do it will chase us and killed us, got it Joey.

But what do we eat, I am so, so hungry and I am willing to eat those wild berry, you need to know which one are the good one, if you don't it will kill you.

No, yours not going eat them and you will died if you do, and I want you to be alive and you mean too much too me and I want to survive this and I want went we get back to civilization that we get married and go on a honeymoon far from here, do hear what I am saying you are my life and I want to comes here for adventure and I didn't think it was going comes out this ways, Karen.

I do understand what you saying and I just want be together and don't make me cried, don't leave me, I won't and Joey came up to her and kiss her lips and said let go into the tent and we will be fine and the morning we will walks some more and we will get home, I promise you with my heart.

I know my heart is near your heart and you are my world and I want to be with you all my life, Karen and Joey kissed and that night they make love and then they fell asleep in each arms and the next day they pack the stuff and carry it and then they stop and looks around and they heard elephants sound and then they saw Monkeys in the trees and Karen said we are going the right way and we will soon sees the road that I took before, we are very near the river.

I just remember and we will soon see a village and those peoples will help us and then we will get back to "Cape Town' and then we can eat and get a shower and pack and then take a flight home, honey one thing, we lost our tickets and we have no money and our family will wire the money and we will be fine, you know that your family was against me, by taking you to Africa, do you think that they will help us after the big fight that we had and you said that you don't want to see them again, I know what you saying but I will apology to family and they will forgive and everything will be fine.

Hope that you are right, I don't want to be stuck in Africa and one thing I hope that I didn't get fired from my job, because I suppose to be in the office about three weeks ago, I know and about me?

Later that they day, walk through the jungle and ran into few snakes and some try to bite them and they killed them and squeeze venom out and had raw snake and even they had some fruit and Joey said I am feeling better and Karen said we need to looks out from cheetah and leopards and tigers, and he said, I know and most of all "quicksand" yes and other dangerous, and wild animals, I do hear you loud and clear.

Suddenly stop and Joey said I hear something and Karen said what?

It is coming our way and I think it is an lion and you must hide and I will tried to fight it off and no are crazy? No but I am trying to save our lives, and you are trying to get killed and leaving alone in the jungle and I am going to fight it with you, do you hear what I am saying? Yes I do and you are a stubborn woman, that why I love you.

"Watched out it coming and it going to attack us, and Joey pick up a twig and Karen said you must be nut to kill the lion, with a twig. Where is the gun that Ben had? I don't know if probably without bullets, but it is a better chance of fight.

Come on Karen, I will hurt the lion, no you will not the only thing that you will do is get him more angry, so we will have an fighting chance by using a gun.

I have never seen you this ways and Karen said I just want to get home in one piece, don't you, yes I do and so we will looks for the gun and shoot the lion.

That is the plan and so you are on my, page Joey, yes and so Karen search for gun but it was not in the tent and then she thought it probably in Ben backpack, and Karen looks and found it and said now we have a fighting chance. Your right Karen…

CHAPTER 25

Karen took out the gun but no bullet and now what? I am looking for them it is roaring toward us and we need to shoot it now, I cannot I don't the bullets.

Just run Karen and I will be in back you and Karen said no I am not running and then she found one bullet and put into the pistol and aim at the lion and but didn't take the shot and Joey said what are waiting for?

Karen said if the lion come toward us and tried to attack and then I will shoot the lion, but if the lion goes back into the jungle I will not killed it.

Now who is nut here now? I can you say that about me, I came back for you and I just wanted to save you and you are treated me like shit and what wrong with you?

Then Karen walk away and said, I am bit angry with you and I want to speak with you and you can be on your own, and she kept on walking and then she heard Joey screaming for help and she ran toward him and the lion was about to bite him and she pull the trigger and kill the lion and Joey said well you took your time to save me, thanks a lot. You should be happy that I came back, I am, you would have left me, but I didn't and so I came back and his clothes were torn and a bit of blood on his knee and Joey got up with a limp and Karen hold him up and he was appreciate that were not torn into piece by the lion.

Now Joey wanted to apologize and Karen said what you said I am not sure that I don't believe what you saying, I think went we get back we should go separate way, you don't mean it, yes I do and you don't listen to what I am saying and sometime you just act like an child, so you are saying that you seen my true colors, yes you can be an liar and cheat.

I have never cheat on you and I always love you, and Karen said but you were mean to me, and I didn't like it and I have nothing else to say.

We are still in the jungle and we are still hungry and we are very exhaust and we should stop picking on each other and we should wait until we get back home and not now.

We are confuse and we are stranded in the jungle with the wild life and any minute we can end up dead, so we should just relax and focus to get out of her and before making any final decision, yes you are right.

About half hour later Joey put up the tent and then the rain came and thunder and lighting and Karen got very close to Joey and hold his hand and then they kissed and but they heard growling and branches breaking and something was coming really close and Karen said I am out of bullets. Just run and don't looks back and it might not follow us, it will and just keep running.

Then they stop and he said it is clear and said I want to hold you and I also want to says I really need you in my life when we make it out here alive I want to with you forever, then they kissed and he and she close their eyes and then Joey lay her on the ground and was near and said I want to be with you, so do I, just hold tight and then they heard an "roar" and Joey said we better get up hurried and I think that you should climb the tree, what? You heard what I said, yes but it is ridicules and just do It., fine I will.

Karen said are coming up to the tree and he said no but I will try to get that beast away from here and you are risking your life so come up too me now and don't do it, please I need you, I know you do, that why I am doing it.

About an minute later, an lion just roar right in and was chasing Joey in the jungle so Karen climb down and try to follow Joey but she doesn't sees him and a piece of his tee shirt on the ground and no sight of him and the lion.

Karen keeps on walking and walking and she looks around, and thought to herself and says where is Joey, and then she found his one shoe and trace of blood and now she know not good sign.

Karen looks around and now she sees lions staring at her and Karen think not to run but slowly walks away and not looking into their eyes, but Karen holding a gun in her hand and was ready to shoot but remember no bullet, and said shit. Now she know that the lions are licking there paws and staring right at her and now Karen walk away and once again, the lion follow her and then out of the bushes Joey jump out and disaster the Lions and Karen run into the jungle and then she sees an hyenas and they were hungry and they wanted to eat her and Karen started to fight with one and stick a knife into the hyena and the blood bleed to the ground and at that moment she thought they were attack her but they when after the dead hyena and she walk and was relief at that moment and went back to Joey but Joey was fine and they both walks and walks for mile, and then a tribe jump out of the jungle and drag them to the tribe camp and they were tied up and no chance to get loose and the tribe was speaking in a foreign language and Karen said now we are going to die here.

No we are not, then helicopter flew over and the tribe was scare and ran off

CHAPTER 26

The tribe was gone and Karen said well maybe that was an search party and about a minute later, Karen and Joey loose and walking in the jungle and then they saw an jackals and roaming the jungle and now Joey and Karen were terrify for their life and Karen said just keep on walking and Joey said I am exhaust and tired and I want to rest and not now, I bit further, and Joey said fine, I am something to drink like "water" and Karen said okay but a bit not a lot we need to ratio how we drink, got it.

They were more closer to the river and then Karen said now we put up our tent and in the morning we will fish and hunt for foods and find some water and Karen said I think I sees the "waterfall" we will get our supply" and we are still ratio our foods and water do you understand? Yes Karen, seem like you know what you are doing? Guess so, but I never did things like this before in my life and it is an new experience, and I don't dislike it but I just want to survive this ordeal and get home and I am worry that it might not happen.

So Karen and Joey talk near the fire and Joey said I told you this were be an adventure but not this long, yes I know but we are together and we love each other, and so Karen goes into the tent and change her dirty clothes and find some tiger short and top and Joey said well I didn't know that you had clean clothes and she said, well I bought them went I was looking for you.

I really think that you are so hot and not now, we need to figure out how to get out the jungle and then in the dark, she heard an "roar" and a minute later, Joey was gone, and drag away and she looks around, that the tiger jump on him and drag him away and now Karen was alone in the jungle.

Now Karen was thinking, I am alone and I cannot fight the wild animals. Tigers and Lions and hyenas and jackals and what will I do now?

Karen was in a panic of her life and now she wandering what will happen now?

So Karen thought the night she will stayed in the tent and tomorrow she will make wooden stick with a knife to defense her life and will stayed in the cave.

I will make a vine that I can swing from one tree to another and she thought that was a good idea but now she was on her own.

Now she realize all decision that she make will keep her alive, and no mistake to be made and she just lay in the tent and keep her eyes open for tigers lions and other predators in the jungle and then she felt a something was crawling up her leg and it was a snake and it was brown and red stripes and Karen knew it was poison snake and she pull out the spear and stab it and then there was another one and now she killed two poison snake and took out the venom and cut it up and decided to eat it raw and skin it off and she chew and chew it and then she took a drink of water and close her eyes and fell asleep and the next morning she got her stuff and started to walk to the cave and then a little brown monkey follow her and she started to called it "Chocolate chip" and the monkey stayed on her side and they both stayed together and at night Karen went into the cave with a fire going and sat there and thought of Joey.

But she heard someone calling out her name and she when out and it was Joey, in blood and so she drag him inside and Karen said I thought you were dead, and he said "Look at me" and she did and she had some rag to wrap up and stop the bleeding and Joey said, you need to go and you cannot stayed, because of the smell of blood they will come and get us, at this point I thought that Joey was delusion and but I didn't listen to him and then it happen that a tiger enter the cave and try to drag Joey out and Karen stab him with the spear and the tiger laid and it seem it was dead but somehow the tiger got up and tried to attack Karen and Joey said go, go now… It will not let me go and the monkey tried to sit on top of Joey and Karen said chocolate chip get off, and Karen said I am not leaving you.

But the tiger was not giving up and was fighting with Karen and she almost fell and Joey somehow got up and then Joey was drag off and lines of blood out the cave and Karen couldn't do anything at this point and now she knew that she saw the eye of the tiger and she knew it was vicious and a killer. Karen stayed in the cave and live there and also find vine to hang from tree to tree and she just knew how to survive and now the she was getting really friendly with the wild animals they are becoming her friends, and she started to like living in the jungle and picking fruits and making straw skirt and she was like so happy and no more stress and having her monkey "Chocolate chip" on the side of her and then a lion, became friendly to her and she was petting it and feeding what she had and then Karen just hang out in her cave and water by the river where a crocodile tried to bite her, so she stayed away from there and once in a while snake came by and she threw the knife stab it and so she had some snake some fishes and took shower in the waterfall and had an flowers in her hair and then she just had a fire at her campsite and didn't think about the loss of Joey and her mind was just being in the jungle and waking up, and under the stars and she knew that she was more restless and didn't even think on moving on, and just living near the river and the waterfall.

CHAPTER 27

Time when by and now it is like one year and Karen still out in the wilderness and Karen, sat near the fire, then she thought about Joey with his hat and it was tan and he was tall and every night Karen thought of him but it was like fading away and but once in the while, and bee and the butterfly and, I dust off and I got up and I was not giving up on life and I am going survive.

In the past I bite my tongue and I didn't says anything what I thought, but when I fell and I dust myself off and I felt that I accomplished what and I feel like an champion and it felt good, even though I am alone in the jungle and now it is about a year and I have not seen my family so. So that why I need to know what I am doing and not to be drag by a tiger or hyena to eat me up.

Sometime I visit the elephants and they spray me down like a hose and, and cool me off and that is my day in the jungle where I lives.

When the sun comes out I go into the waterfall and I just get wet and I feel cool and when the night comes I go into the cave and I have the fire going and I just sit and then I fall asleep and I do think about being home with my family and I know one day they will find me.

I have a journal that on my first day of the safari and I didn't know I would be alone here and I thought that Joey were be here but the tiger took him away from me and now I am just a brave woman in the jungle and one of these day, someone will comes and they will found me.

Then Karen close her eyes and fell asleep and nears the bat were flying above her head and but Karen didn't hears them and then the next morning Karen make more spear and to catch fish and protection herself from the wild cats around her.

Then one day it rain and it was about 25 inches and I didn't know went it was going to stop and that day I stayed in the cave with my monkey a "Chocolate Chip" and the friendly tiger beside me, I felt safe at that moment but I had the fear what is out there and so I will wait for someone to rescue me from this jungle and I just want to be home with my family, and I have lost my cell phone went Leo stole our money and our passport and I don't know, if I will be allow to leave Africa went they found me.

But I am not giving up hope and I know one day I will be home and I hope my little dog "is okay, and I am saying I miss you snowball and wish stayed home with you and hope that my parents are okay! They must be worried sick about me, and I do think of them and I know I will be fine.

Later that day Karen heard sound of the jackal and Karen had the fear that they might attack and be torn into pieces, but Karen had a plan to climb up on the tree, went it stop rainy and so it will be a caution and safely of be safe.

But the rain continue to rain and I was afraid that I would probably get flood away to somewhere else and but I just pray to god, and I do have a pet a tiger that with me and it make sure, I don't get hurt.

"Eye of tiger" that roar and sometime want to run but this tiger is so friendly and I don't feel threaten not all.

Later today I will go hunter for foods and my tiger and my monkey will be on my side and so, and I will walk a mile away from here and I don't see anyone kept the two animal beside me and once time I seen the crocodile in the water and I just ran and I thought it were follow me but didn't.

Sure my life is not the same, since I left Manhattan and I was a city girl and now I became a girl that is not afraid to try anything new he convince me to comes to "Africa" to take the safari and I didn't have a good feeling about it but I did want to be with him, so I came and now I am alone and he got torn up into piece by a vicious tiger that drag him from the campsite and now I need to survive and found my way back to "Cape town" and then I can called my family and tell them I am alive.

For now I need hunt for food and swing on the vine and the trees and try not to get bitten by the brown red stripe snake, if I do I will died in the jungle.

Karen walk to the waterfall and wet herself and then she saw a few elephants and then Karen pet the elephants and they follow her to the camp and then she just lay under the sun and monkey lay right next to her.

Monkey then lay on top of her stomach and then the tiger came on her side and then Karen fell asleep and then hurt some gun fire and it make the tiger a little stress and started to growl and running around the campfire and now I was in a little panic and so I just stood still and didn't move at all and now.

It seem like an fire burning and now I am very, very terrify what will happen to me, and will they come and take me, will be send to some sex traffic gang.

CHAPTER 28

I hid from them and I saw there pointed gun and I try to keep the monkey and the tiger quiet, but the tiger when out of the camp and then I heard a shot and I was still hidden from the hunters and I saw one with a brown hair and about 5 feet and 9 inch tall and he was medium build and had a scar on his left cheek and I knew that if they found me, I would be probably rape and kills or send to some peoples sell me at the trade market and I had no bullet to shoot them and get away, because there would too many of them and I was alone.

About one hour they looks around and I had the fire out and so they just pass my camp and I was relief for a second I thought the man with the beard would come this ways and hid and make sure that I would not an sound.

Later that day, when the coast was clear, I got up from the ground and when into the cave and then I looks around and then I when to the waterfall and got clean and just looks around and it was safe and then I look for my tiger and the only I saw was blood on the ground and the tiger was drag from that location and I couldn't find him.

I walks back to camp and I was scare to death, I had a pack of lions standing here my cave and I didn't have a chance to climb the tree and now, I couldn't run and I didn't see my monkey, once again I was alone and I was the only one that had to fight them, but I was overwhelm with the situation and things were getting crucial and I had no choice, and I knew that I had to live and not die.

Then I heard more shot were fire and then I couldn't hide but the man with black hair and mustache saw me and he put the finger the lips and said be quiet and you will be safe, but he was not like those other men.

He had a sparkle in his eyes and he was handsome and he was a hunter, and I was never attractive to that type of men, but I felt the chemistry from far way.

A minute I saw the man and then he gone and I was looking and I did want to get out of the jungle and I knew that I was taking a bit risk at that moment.

I turned back and he was standing under the tree and I said, watched out I see a snake coming and he took out his knife and killed the snake and I walk up and he said my friend will comes back soon, you must hide and then he asked do you need to get help and she answered quietly yes, and I don't have a phone and when I get to town I will make a called but I won't let my friends know. Thanks and he asked her name and she said my name is Karen and he said my name is Pete, and I am from Florida, the Tampa area, and you I am from New York, and she walks away and they were coming back.

So Pete walk away, and said hide my friends will comes and they will catch you and but I will comes back for you when they are sleeping, ok, I will be alone. I will take you out of here and you will be able to contact your family and get home and Karen said will it be a bit risk for you yes it will be but don't worry about it and I will sneak out and get too you and I will show you, and Karen said, you will not harm me? No, and I will be fine so will you, and she said yes and it will be good being home with my family.

"Then he left and Karen when into the cave and didn't looks back and just sat on the ground and then took her sleeping bag and went to sleep, and meanwhile Pete, met up with his friends and he didn't say anything about Karen and then said, I am a bit tired and he when into his tent and his two friends were knew that Pete was up to something but they didn't know what?

Later that night Pete pretend that he was fast asleep and about one hour later Pete got up and put on his shoes and snuck out and didn't make a sound, but one of buddy was just watching what Pete was doing and so he got up and follow him and then he came back to camp and wake up his friend and said Pete met a girl and he is keeping her for himself, and so we are going to get him and the girl, so that is the plan said Jon to Nick, yes we need to go after him and he cannot keep us in the dark and he need to share this girl with us.

Pete was walking in the jungle and thought that he was alone and about a mile behind him was Jon and Nick, and then he got to Karen and said now we need to leave, and Karen said I need to pack my stuff and Pete said don't tell too long and I hope that no one didn't follow me.

Now they were on their ways out and Pete said to Karen, I know this jungle and we will not get lost and we will be fine, take my word.

So how can you be friends with them they killed innocence animals and you help them, that how I survive.

So I will not argue with you so let keep walking and so they did, and then Pete heard a branch break and Pete said we are not alone here, I think Jon and Nick are here too.

I think we have a problem and they are not friendly like I am so when I tell you too run, you run, do you understand? Of course I do.

CHAPTER 29

Jon and Nick, started to yelled out and said we will catch you and tied you both up and Pete said to Karen don't listen to them, I know the ways out and we will be fine, so follow the "river" and go up toward the mountain and then more up river and after the waterfall and then Karen said I hears gun fire and Pete said they are not too far and they are very near us and don't let them catch us, and Karen just kept on running and then she trip and hurt her ankle and then Pete check her ankle and then said well I will hold you and you will fine, and about two feet away Pete sees Jon and Nick and then were shooting there rifle and Karen said, duck and the shot miss them by an inch.

Now Jon and Nick were getting more pissed about Pete and he betray them and so now they want get revenge toward Karen and Pete.

For a moment Pete stop and Karen said what wrong and he said I think that I got shot in the leg, so you continue to walk toward the road and we will be fine.

Sound like you are trying to convince yourself that we will make to the town, and tell the authority, yes and then you can called your family and Karen said will you comes with me and he said no, I will go back to Jon and Nick and you cannot go back they will killed you. No they won't kill me.

Now do you know, they are my friends and I know them for a long times Karen said I am not going alone, do you hear what I am saying, you will be better off that you, no…I will not go alone, don't hear what I am saying if I go with you they probably killed us both.

You are not scaring me, and when though hell and back and you are my new friend and I am not going to loss you, you don't even know me, I could be bad than those two.

If that true, why are you showing me the ways out, maybe it is a trap and then I get rid of you know no that is not true about you Pete. I believe that you are the good guy and so you will not hurt me, so you are so sure about me?

But they are coming and we need to found a hiding place and do you know any place around here? No I don't said Karen, and I don't where I am.

I hears a car coming this way and some gun going off and then Nick and Jon were yelling and screaming and they are very close, so hide, I think we are going into disaster and I think that they will catch us, so when you sees the bushes move and you run for your life and don't looks back, okay.

Karen ran right into Jon arms and now Karen is screaming and yelling and then Jon said we have your girlfriend, and come and get her and Karen said no don't and go and get help, and then Pete said let her go and I will comes back with you too camp, and then Pete had to put his hands up and they took an rope and tied around there neck and Karen at that moment was frighten and scare about the ordeal that she has too go through with these men.

Karen begged them to let her go and she said I won't tell anyone and about a minute later Jon got attack by an lion and was torn into pieces and Nick was not too far from the lion and the campfire was burning and more lions came and now Nick pull out his rifle and started to shoot and then one jump from the above and Karen somehow untied herself and then untied Pete.

Then Karen put up a wood and place into the fire and then pointed the fire toward the lion and it back way and Pete said you are lion more angry and you need to get away and Karen said no way I am not going to lose you, like lost my boyfriend.

I am a stranger and so I give you permission to leave now and you will be killed into pieces and don't worry about it.

I do and I want you show me the way out and I want you to come along with me, do you get it.

Yes, loud and clear so just move slowly and don't make attention to the lion and just walk slow and Karen said I should stayed at the cave and I was safe there, and I am sorry that I listen to you. Don't you want to get home, yes I do.

Once again Karen walks out, and walk and Pete stayed for a little while and didn't make any attention and the lions were feeding on Jon and Nick and Pete had an opportunity to escape the lions.

When Pete caught up with Karen and Pete said at last we are out of the jungle and Karen was relief and Pete said we have a lot of walking and I know that your ankle hurt and I know that my leg hurt because I got shot and it is bleeding, yes I sees.

When we reach the town we will tell the same story what happen, yes I will tell them that you helped me and Pete said I cannot be with you and I am a wanted man and they will put me into prison and no they won't and I tell them that you save me from those evil men.

They will lock me up and I will take you half way and I will leave you.

CHAPTER 30

No, don't leave me and Pete said I will meet you in New York City and then I will tell the whole truth, but I need to go now.

I will not make It without you, yes you will and stayed whiny and don't act like an child and now Karen was getting a bit angry at him and then he was gone and she looks around and no sight of him and was not too far from "Cape town" and she walk very slow and when she about to reach the town, Karen fell to the ground and some peoples saw her and they ran to her and pick her up and took her inside and then gave her water and foods…

Then they asked what happen she said I got lost in the jungle with my boyfriend and he got killed by a tiger and I see the "eye of the tiger".

They started to asked her questions but she had no answers and she wanted to called her parents and get back home, but they took her to the hospital for observation and she refuse to get the treatment and then she called her parents and they said that they will wire the money and talk to the embassy about getting you home and she was happy to hear about that's and her dad said that he were take the first plane out to Africa.

Karen said no, I don't want to sees anyone right now, but booked me the first flight out and they said we will and then said we are happy that you are fine.

Yes I am, and I should be home a week, and they said yes you will.

Meanwhile Pete was lurking in the back of her and she didn't sees him and he just watched her when she was boarding the plane, but then he snuck in the back way into the plane and was disguise like an old man and he came to her seat and said "miss" can I sit here and she nodded her head and said yes! But she noticed he seem familiar to her but she couldn't put her finger and then the plane was on the runaway and was about to take off he took off the hat and then he smiled at her and she said, you are alive? Yes I got away and I didn't wanted to stay in Africa, and I just wanted to get back home to my roots.

They talk for a while and Pete said you did have an adventure before things started to happen to you and your boyfriend? She nodded her head and said yes and it was awful and I don't want to think or talk about it again and I am glad that I am going home. Later that day, Karen fell asleep and Pete looks over his shoulder and then the thunder and lighting came and the plane shook and shake and Karen slept through it and Pete got an text from one of his buddy, that they will meet at the airport in Kennedy Airport and they asked if he has the merchandise and he said, yes I do and it was easy and I didn't have a problem and she will be with me, and don't let her get suspicion, and she will run and they said we got it.

About one hour later Karen woke up and she said Pete, is it really you? He shook his head and said I have a plan to get you away from the terminal and she said, would you been followed and he said yes and I need to protection and so there will be an black car in front of the terminal and you go right in and it will take you home and Karen trusted him and so she did what he told her and so, the plane was about to land in five minutes and Karen said go into the black BMW, yes and it will take you home, okay I will.

"Then the phone rang and Pete answer it and said, it coming together" and then he hung up when Karen approach him, but someway Karen didn't trust him totally, so she took a walk in the aisle and sees what he was doing and then she came back and asked who were you talking too? Just my mom and dad and then and they will comes and get me from the airport and now Karen knew that Pete was lying and she could tell by looking into his eyes.

The plane landed and Karen sat for a while and Pete was in a hurried to get off and he said Karen come on, let go now and Karen said I need to called my parents and tell that I will be home soon!

But he took the phone away from her and Karen said what going on here and I just want to talked to you before you go home and she said so you are going to tell me lies, I never lies too you and I save you from those evil men.

So Karen got up and when with him and said, no funny business and he said, I got you out of Africa and this is how you thanks me?

Okay, tell me what going down and follow me to the car and when I tell you to run, you run, okay, they think that I am working with them but I am not.

You are the only that can save my life from them, you would the target in Africa from day one and now they want you, and they want to sell you for the highest bidder, so you are saying that they want to sell me to an slave traffic market? Yes, you got it! They were walking out the terminal and then Pete got knock down on the ground and Karen kept on walking and someone in back of her grab her and pulls her into the black car and put a cloth over her mouth and Karen was out.

The next morning Karen woke up in a wooden box with punch hole and she couldn't really sees much and so she tried to yelled out and one man came and hit her on the hands and said be quiet, I will killed you, please let me go!

Karen knew that she was still near the airport and she knew that somehow she needed to escape and but she didn't have a plan, but Karen was frighten and scare and then she heard Pete voice and one of the man was beating him up and he was bleeding and they said, you have double cross us and you will died.

I have not double cross who said that they are liars. Let me go, my uncle will be angry at you if you don't let me go!! Well your uncle is dead we killed him and he will not care what happen to you, then he looks and his uncle came in and he said you have betray our family with this girl. I have not uncle, I did delivery her and what else to do want from me. I did your dirty work and this is my reward, of being punish? You don't tell order and you are just out of control and we are not good to be in or organization, you got it Pete. Then Pete tried to plead with his uncle to let the girl go and her family known that she was in this plane and the security camera will be shown has a kidnapped of Karen.

Karen started to cried and said my family will pays any amount of money and please let me go, but know one listen to Karen and they continue to bargain the sale of Karen to the highest bidder in Cape Town.

Meanwhile that Pete was tied up on a hook and he was turning his wrist to get loose and rescue Karen and he was thinking how he will take the gun away his so called friends, so he got one hand loose and it was a cut and bleeding and now he needed to get the second loose and get the gun. That was his plan and so, and he had to pretend that he was still hook up and now for the distract, that Pete will do a sneak attack behind of the men. But Pete didn't want to get shout and he just want to get Karen and he just needed to find out where they took and so he got the first man down and got the gun and he knew that they were near the boat dock in a storage and he needed to go and get her out of box and so he knew that time was running out and he tried to do an diversion get out of himself and so he did, so got some firecracker and lit them off and about three men came and he knock them with an karate kick and then one of men he hold him by the neck and said, tell me where Karen is? If you don't I will break your neck and so he said she is in storage 123 and it will be leaving the dock at noon and you have only five minutes and you will not make it and then he said which ship are they using, and he said If I tell you they will killed me, I will killed you if you don't tell me.

He said the ship name is fairy white, and that is a usually name for a ship

CHAPTER 31

Then he just broke his neck of that man and ran off and when outside and no one was watching, so he snuck out and got into a black car and drove like a mad man and he knew that time was ticking way and he wanted to save her.

Meanwhile Karen was yelling and screaming and one of the man when to her and open the box and she thought that she going to be free and about a minute later she got pinch on the finger and fell inside the box and he close it shut and someone came to the storage and it is time to take the package to the ship now.

They took the box and boarded on the ship and Pete was driving out of control to catch and he was not sure which dock and where the package was going but he didn't give up and about ten minutes the ship sail and it was heading to Africa and Pete got to the dock and the ship was gone and now he thought that he has to get somehow to get on that ship and then he thought well I am going to rent a copter and I will get Karen back.

Five hours pass and then Karen woke up and he was in the bottom of the ship and Karen thought, now I will probably dies here and so she just sat there and didn't give up for that moment of time.

About eight hour later, Pete got the copter and was flying over New York City and headed to New Jersey and knew that he would find them and call the coast guard and stop that ship before it reaches foreign waters.

Pete was over and over and he could find it and now he just wander where they are and then he saw the ship and called the coast guard and told them what was going on and he they alert the police water patrol and now they were following the ship and so the water patrol and they got to the ship and there would shooting and backward and forward a few bad guys got shots and some police got hurt at this, and then Pete from the copter he jump into the water and swam to the ship and said I was the one report about the kidnap and they let him on and he search for Karen and he when to the last floor of the ship and found the box and he open it will a screwdriver and Karen was not alert at that moment and Pete said the ordeal is over and you are going home.

About ten minutes later, Pete got hit on the head and Karen was pull out of the ship to a ship and when Pete got up and said where is she? One of the officer said her uncle took her home, why did you let him take her?

He was not her uncle he was one of the bad guy and now she might be lost forever, and he walk off the ship and on to the dock.

She was yelling and screaming and he said missy I will make you be quiet and you will not like it she tried to bite him and he push her on the floor and he said I cannot damage you because I am getting a lot of money for you.

Why don't you let me go mister my family gives you has much money the bidder.

Well, they will give me one million dollars and diamond. I am not about diamond and I won't tell anyone about you.

Missy we are headed to Africa and you will have a good life with MR. Snow, and he will treated you well and so, I don't want to say anything do you hear me?

Do you want a tape over your face and so she said no I don't so shush and Karen kept quiet, but thought how to escape.

The he had a gun in back of her and said don't make any attention and I will shoot you and I won't even blink, and she said you will being found and you will end up in prison and for a long time, and they were entering the terminal and headed to the private jet and Pete is trying to figure out where is Karen and his uncle and at this point he just stop and think and Karen and the uncle are boarding the private jet and then Pete remember the plane, so run out of the storage and some of the goons try to shoot him and so Pete, just knock them out and take the keys and get into the car and hurried to the terminal A, and drive up and hit the curb and then the police chase him and he said "shit" and I cannot get caught and he stop the car and jump out and run into the terminal and looks for the private plane and it is on the runaway and Karen said you will not get away with this, missy I am getting away and just sit down and shut your mouth, I will shutting for.

The plane take off and Pete said to the lady at the desk and said can books a first flight to Africa and so he said so how much do I owe?

It is about three thousand, and he said, here is my credit card and she said I need an ID to prove that is you and he did shown it and then she printed the ticket and the boarding pass.

About half hour later in the flight Karen said you will be found and punished and I will tell them what you did to me, and they will get you and you will be sorry and then he said, be quiet you bitch.

Then he make few called and when inside and took the steering and it was on autopilot and now Karen was alone in the seat and now she was thinking of plan.

CHAPTER 32

So she kept her down and try to untied herself and about ten minutes later, the uncle came back and saw that she was trying to get loose and so he put a cloth over her face and when back to fly the plane and then the plane was having mechanical problem and one of the engine stop and he started up and then the plane was going down straight down and Karen woke up and said what going on and he said buckle up now, are we going to dies?

No, and Karen was terrify and scare at that moment and now she didn't think about running away but praying of staying alive.

Now Pete was boarding the plane and the Police were not too far from and Pete was worry that they might catch him and he will not be able to rescue Karen.

Then he was relief that they didn't sees him and so Pete got on the plane and put his head on the pillow and hid from the police and so then everyone got the plane and it took off and Pete needed to contact someone to help him and the one that he trusted was Lee, and he got Lee on the phone and explains the situation…

So I be waiting for them to land and I will follow them and I will tell you the location of the sale.

I owe you big time and then Lee waited for the plane and it never came and they got the report that the plane was off radar, at that moment, the Karen was sitting and then a minute the plane crash into the jungle and the Pete, uncle instant dies and she just got cuts and bruises and walk out and then the plane explosion in flame and Karen, almost pass out and then started to walk into the jungle and it was getting dark and now Karen was alone in South Africa, and no one to help her. No foods and no water and she kept walking and walking and got further from civilization and then her family got notify that the plane crash and no survivor.

Went Pete heard that he said she cannot be dead and I will be landed in half hour and I do want to go to the crash sights and Lee said are you sure, they will not let us in and I need to know that they found her body.

Karen family will becoming tomorrow and Pete said no, I am going to go now to the crash sights and I know that she didn't perish in the crash, I just feel it.

Pete went and it was tied up with yellow tape and he said can I comes and sees crash and they said no you are not allow and so he somehow snuck inside and then he said don't you sees those footprints? It could be Karen and he could be in the jungle and you must let me search for her, stayed back or we will shoot.

I am trying to save her and you are stopping me, please I am begged you to let me go, and find her and she could be hurt and bleeding and they said no, and so Pete tried to go another way and so they caught him and Karen just kept on walking and walking and so she stop and she was hurt and confuse, an then she lay down and slept, until morning and she heard elephants sound nears by and she walks toward them and there was about ten of them and even a baby elephants and she wanted to pet them but she was afraid and so she didn't.

The next morning Pete when back to the city and rented a car and starting to search for Karen, and but he had no luck at all.

Pete search for Karen from morning to night and he didn't find her yet!

Meanwhile Karen was near a waterfall and near a cave and Karen pick up two stick to start a fire and her hand was cut and a little bleeding and dripping on the ground, and now Karen is being shadow by an jackal and then she saw an leopard and now Karen doesn't have anything to defense herself, and now she tried to hide in the bushes, but she heard an growl and it is really near, and then she wrap her arm with a torn tee shirt and the bleeding stop, and then seem like they left and now Karen rub too stick to make an fire and it a bit cold and Karen just sit there and think what her name?

Pete, at the hotel and take out a map and make circle where he should search a new location, and that evening Karen, saw the "Eye of the tiger" and Karen thought it were attack her, and near the water, she saw crocodile and was about to grab her leg and she ran way and then she when back and sat near the fire and fell asleep and then something jump on her shoulder and it was an cute little monkey and she started to scream and then it came on her lap.

Pete left his room and when into his car with couple weapons and the map and he when toward south instead of east, and he thought maybe Uncle Bob was taking her to South Africa, and he drove and drove, and he had to stop and he couldn't go further with the car and then he had walk the rest of the way, but he called Karen Parents and said, I will find your daughter and I will bring her home, and they said, we will be waiting for your called and then they hung up and then Pete when into the jungle and he knew it were not be easy, because he was in the wilderness, and a lot wild cat and dangerous snakes are very poisonous.

But he also knew that he loved Karen and wanted her and gets her home and he just blame himself, getting her in the situation with his uncle Bob.

Pete walks about 3 miles and then set up a camp and stayed overnight and would do the search in the morning, and Karen just was too exhaust and fell asleep with the monkey and was like shriving and shaking, and but slept the whole night, the next morning Karen got up and looked around and she thought too herself that she have go near the water to wash up and so she did and a minute later, the crocodile, tried to bite her and she pull away and she ran to the cave, and sat there and had tears in her eyes.

Now she was started to remember the kidnapped and taking the plane to South Africa, now Karen had fear in her eyes that the kidnapped will comes back and she will be stole to the highest bidder. So Karen decided to take the shower under the fall and she washed her face and clothes at the same time.

Pete got up and pack his stuff and headed toward Karen, that what he thought, then, Pete was being follow by an Lion and he would not stop following him and so he didn't run to make the lion, chase him and also had to be careful of quicksand, is very near and he knew that known one save him.

One hour Pete was in the deeper of the jungle and he looks around everywhere and he couldn't find Karen, and he thought I probably when the wrong ways.

Then he saw something and he just follow the path and he felt that he was getting closer of finding her.

Meanwhile Karen heard sound in the bushes and now she was going to hide in the cave and not to make a sound.

Pete was approaching the waterfall and the cave and he was going to looks in side and then he walk in and she hit him and he fell to the ground.

One hour later, he woke up and said why did you hit me? I thought it was one of the thugs that were after me, and I am sorry I hurt you.

I came to get you home and to your family and then he got close to her and said can I kiss you? And then they kissed.

CHAPTER 33

Then he hold her tight and took out some clothes for her to change and so she went and changed them, and we will be leaving in half hour and so we will be taking the flight to Newark, and she said will my family be there and he said yes they will be this time.

He smiled at him and said thank you for coming to get me and I cannot wait to get back home, and he said this time I will be boarding the plane with you and I have clearance with the government of Africa and I am not an threaten.

Pete said that we will be walking about 3 miles to the car and she said it is fine and I will be able to do it.

We will stop for a moment and then continue walking and it will not be stress for you and Karen said no, I will be fine.

Time when by and they stop and then they continue and Karen spotted an lion and now Karen was scare, that they were be attack, and Pete said don't worry we will be just fine, and she just looking in back her and saw the lions and coming toward them, and she said are sure that we will be fine? He nodded his head and said yes, we will be fine, and they walks through the jungle and he said be careful of the snakes, and she said, I know, but then Karen trip and fell and he said are you okay? She said, I feel that I sprain my ankle and he said that is not good and so he got her a big branch and told Karen to hold on and she did and they were not too far from the car.

Pete said I think I when the wrong way, and Karen said no, I want to get out of here now, we will and then he said, we will be walking near quicksand, and watched your step, I will and you too.

Now he tried to make a called and tell someone that they are coming to the airport and the signal was not working and Pete just kept to himself and then he said I think that I see the car, and now Karen was relief and she was going home to her family, and Pete said hope that you won't forget me?

Karen said, don't says that I will sees you, you will be on the flight, and he said, sure I will be but when we get to the New York City, I still want too sees then too,

Even though my Uncle Bob, put you through and you still want to see me! Yes he was your uncle but you save me and I really appreciate what you did.

Suddenly a lion jump out and Karen said watched out and Pete said I am fine and so he shot the lions and it echo in jungle and he said I apology that I killed the lion, but if you didn't you would been dead, and you save your life and mine.

So they reach the car and he said get in and now they headed to the road and out of the jungle and to the main road and headed to the airport and make a called and that she is safe and her family was very happy to hear and he made a second called and make reservation the first flight out of Africa.

He shown her that she has a passport and Identity to shown airport and so he told when they arrival to the airport to get line to get on the plane and he were get the print out tickets of them.

It took about 20 minutes and Karen stood there and st to comes and he said we are going to gate A and she said tickets and he shown them too her and then about ten they boarding the plane that was headed to Newark near the window and Pete was right next to her, and th asked if she wanted to watched some Movie, and she said yes, but she decided to watched Katy Perry the with her new song, Roar, and Pete said, I really like that song too.

I feel that you are the champion of this ordeal, stop saying that Pete, I know that I went through a lot of things and I did survive, and you came to rescue and you are the "Champion" no I am not…

The plane was on the runway and Karen and Pete hold each hands and the song" Roar" was playing and Karen and Pete kissed one more time and then the plane when up and they were up in 50 thousand feet above Africa and the flight attendance asked if Karen wanted something to eat and she said yes and to drink and Pete had his head on her shoulder and fast asleep.

Karen couldn't wait to get back home but the flight was long and Karen just looks around and known one she knew and so she fell asleep and couple hour came the plane was going to land and it had some mechanical problem with the shaking and then they were very close to Newark and now Karen was looking out the window and said I am home, and about few minute the plane landed and go to the boarding deck and the "Captain Will" said hope that you enjoyed the flight and be safe and hope that you will travel with us again.

Then he parked the plane and everyone was getting off the flight and Karen said wake up Pete, and he said oh, we are home? Yes we are and meanwhile her family was waiting for her to come out of the plane and so Karen said my family is waiting for me, and he got up from his seat and walks her to the terminal and she saw her family and he said, I will let you go now.

Where are you going? You are staying with me, and folks would like to meet you, even though I was the problem they will forgive you and I did.

Karen ran up to her mom and dad and said, I missed you so much and I do want to introduce my friend Pete, and she looks around and he was gone.

They asked where he did go I don't know mom, but he is a good man, that her mom said got you in trouble in sex traffic for the highest bidder. It was his uncle and not him, I don't understand why you are sticking up with this low life and sure he did save you but he also sold you too his uncle and if the plane didn't crash you been a slave sex girl, I do understand and I know that's but he prove that he is not the bad guy.

He the one that looks for me when I was missing and he did get beat up by his uncle Bob and he did save my life and it count for something, sure.

Then they all walks to the car and Pete was looking and he just saw them leaving and Karen was looking around but couldn't see him., then they got outside and got into the car and drove way and then Pete came outside and they were gone and so he tag down a cab and headed home and so when Karen and her parents got home, they had a surprise party, that she was safe and back home with them, and then Karen said, I need to go to Joey apartment and pack my stuff and her mom and dad said not tonight but we will take you in the morning and Karen said I would like to do alone, and so she stayed for an while and then left to her apartment and Pete was lurking in the street and like following her, but she didn't notice him.

When she step inside of the apartment she close the deadlock and couple lock, and then stare at the picture of her and Joey and then started to cried and says I miss you. Then she when to the bathroom and got her PJ and then she when to the bed and when to sleep and meanwhile Pete was looking and saw the lights were out and so he left and when home.

When Pete got home, and his brother said did you hear what happen to Uncle Bob, and Pete said no so what happen? His plane when down in Africa and he died in the crash. So when did this happen, about four days ago, oh I sees.

Then Pete said I had a long day so I am going to sleep and he when into his bedroom and went to sleep and meanwhile Karen toss and turned.

CHAPTER 34

The next morning Karen started to pack her stuff and also called her landlord that she is moving out and not signing the lease and so she will receive her deposit back and will give her keys back in five days from now and she also need to called her job and tell them that she back.

Also explains what happen and her boss, understood and she was back at work in five day and so she work hard and everything was a bit difficult and she had some persons talking about her and she when up to them and said whatever you have says, saying to my face, and behind my back.

You are getting paranoid and you should be here because of your extension vacation well I didn't plan to get lost in the jungle and then kidnaped.

Cindy and Laurie just walk away and Karen was called in to Mr. Brown office and said, I do not want any out bursts in the office, do you understand?

Yes, Mr. Brown, it won't happen again and so she walk out and did her work and Cindy and Laurie, just were staring at her, and then she got a phone called and it was Pete.

Karen said hello, and known one answer and she was about to hang up and he said, hi, this is Pete, do you remember me? Of course I do.

Then he said meet me at the coffee shop around at the corner from your office, and how do you know where I work, so I follow you this morning, oh!

So you are my stalker now no! I am your friend, hope that we can be? Sure we can Karen SAID and so meet me for coffee, and she said I will sees you LATER.

Later that day Karen hurried up to leave the office and meet Pete for coffee and she was excited and so she called her mom and said that she was going out with friend and not to stayed up, and her mom said, don't comes in to late, and Karen said I am not an child and I do care for myself.

When she arrive at the coffee shop, Pete had a rose red and he handed over to her and then Pete gave her a kiss on the lips and she kissed him back.

That night Karen and Pete talk and talk about their and so Pete said, you would have married Joey? She nodded her head and said yes he was love of my life but tragedy that the tiger jump at him and drag him away and that was the last time that I saw him. Joey told me on adventure that I will never forget he was good to me and so I just really missed him and I am not sure that I can have a new relationship with anyone right now, because the grief of losing Joey. I do hear what you are saying, then Karen said I do have feeling for you and I know that we have a connection, from the first day that we met, under weird circumstance, and you were helping your uncle to sell me to the slave market and I don't know if I could even forgive you, but you were torture and you did save me in the jungle and so just give sometime and so, and then Karen got up and said I need to go now... Pete said hope that I can sees you again, but now I am trying to put my life back together.

Karen just walk out and left the red rose on the table and Pete wanted to catch her and then he just stop and walk back to the coffee shop and had a black cup of coffee, and then the phone rang and it was his brother Mike and said, mom is waiting for dinner and he said I will be on my ways home.

But Pete felt that someone was watching him and it was a suspicious character that works for his uncle and so he was very careful, and he needed to warn Karen, about that man.

Karen got home and her mom said so who did you meet tonight and said well my coworker and she said I can tell when you are lying to me, and then Karen said I meet Pete, oh, he is trouble one and I told you not too see him, I am not an child and I can see whoever I want. Don't you remember what happen and he is not good to you and he is" trouble" no he is not he is the one got me home and he told the authority about the sex traffic, and he is not involve with that bracket anyone and he got an job and her mom said you believe what he is saying too you? Yes and I do trust him, and then her cell rang and she answer and it was Pete and he warn her that they are watching you and he said be careful and I will not be around, if I stayed you will not be safe, so I am leaving and I am saying goodbye, no, you can and a minute late he hung up and she said, I am going to my room and her mom we didn't finished this discussion and she said, you don't have worry anymore, he left town, and her mom said good riddle, and how can you says that's!

Karen when into her room and when on the internet and post a photo of herself looking for an attractive man and he should be about 5ft 8 inch and slim and no mustache and dark skin, completion and she put email and half naked photo of herself and then she started to search for an apartment in Manhattan, and two bedroom and roommate.

Then she went into the bathroom and took a shower and couldn't stop thinking of Pete. Then she step out the shower and when into her bedroom and pick her cell and called Pete. But he didn't answer the phone and it said out of service.

CHAPTER 35

Later that night Karen dreamt about him and didn't want to forget him and so the next morning Karen got up for work and was a bit angry about her mom and then she said I will be looking for an place to live and her mom said you have a place to live, well I didn't live in this house for five years when I move in with Joey, don't you remember and she said, Yes but Joey is not alive and you came back home, just temporary and do hear what I am saying mom? Don't be so nasty to you mom and I am not but I am not a child so, I will be on my own.

Your dad will not like that, well I will do want I want and I will not be control and you understand what I am saying mom. And I will be fine. I know you will be…I am on my way to work and her mom asked do you want to have some bacon and scramble eggs and Karen said I will be late for work, and I will sees you later and she left and shut the door and Karen mom called out here is an sandwich I make for you, thanks!

Karen walk out to her steps and walk down and when to the sidewalk and tag and taxi cab and said take me to fifth avenue in a hurried.

"When Karen arrive to the office and step inside the elevator" and press 2309 floor and headed to her office and one of friend Liza called out and said someone in the office got kidnapped and she said who?

I think that Rose was kidnaped in the garage and known one where she is and is she about your height and weight? I don't know.

Then Karen rush out the office and went to her boss and told him that she is resigning from her job and Karen said she still under stress and that why she is leaving and her boss said why don't take leave of absent and but Karen refuse and left the office that day and known one heard from her and she left and move away from New York city and move to Miami, Florida and met a man a name Josh and they hit it off and Karen work at the dress shop and she like the hours and she once in a while called her parents and told the parents that she will be getting married to Josh and Karen said hope you and dad will comes and it will be a month, from today and they said they were tried to comes and they were not happy about Karen being in a collision course by meeting a man two week and getting married and they knew that was an mistake and then Karen when back to work and Karen told her new friends about Josh, and her friend Delores told her that Josh is an player.

But Karen refuse to listen what they were saying and one thing Josh is in the family business and she didn't know what kind, and she also does not know his cousin is Pete. One day Karen was walking near the beach and she thought that she saw Pete but she was not sure but then she said no ways.

Later that day, Josh said that he is leaving on business and the wedding will be postponed for three month and I will be out of the country that all I will says so I will be your wife and you are keeping secrets from me, well you are not my wife yet! He wanted to hit her and she just ducks her face and said, go, and go and leave me alone.

Josh pack and left and said, I think we should just forget about the wedding because I believe you really don't love me, and I will be coming back, because I asked you where yours going? No, I just don't feel it, and it not you but it me, and I don't have time to explained it, just go and I and she slams the door behind him and then toss our things out of the door and lock it.

Two hour later Karen when to work with tears in her eyes and her friend, Delores said what wrong? Well you would right about this man, he just broke up with me by asking questions and he didn't like it.

I know that he was keeping secrets and so I am better off without him, Delores, yes you are and did I tell you that he wants to hit me and I just bend down and he miss me, good that you are not with him anymore.

Then Karen got a block called and she answered and then listens to the voice and it was Pete, and now Karen was happy to hear from him. Karen didn't know what to says to talked with him or just hanged up and he said don't hang up I need to talk with you and sees you, at first Karen said no.

Then she change her mind and he said meet me at the beach at noon and she said, okay I will be there.

Later that day, Karen got into her BMW and drove to the beach and park the car and walk the ways and Pete was waiting at the stand by bar.

She walk up and she was really angry and furious at him and said you left me a year ago and you didn't even called me and then he said you met my cousin and you were going to get marry to him, so I stayed away and so are still with Josh? No, we broke up today, and you probably find out, no I just took a chance, and I do want to be with you, no it will not work, how you know it won't. well you left me and you didn't give me a chance to love you and you just took off and I don't if yours going and you just can decided just take off.

CHAPTER 36

No, I won't and you are just saying that to make me think that you really care about me and Pete said I do care for you and Karen said why did you leave me, that day that you bought me back to my family, I knew that your family would not approve of me, you told me that you love me and you walk away and my life change when I met you Pete, but I am not going to be your girlfriend, in the past you had a chance but now, I don't think so, and Pete said we need to talks more and Karen said I am done talking with you and she walk away and Pete just stood there and wanted to called her back, but she was all ready by her car and was going inside and Pete wave and she didn't sees it.

Then Pete walks on the boardwalks and thinking about Karen and how he wanted to be with her and he need to figure out how to get her back.

Meanwhile Karen on her way home she started think about Pete and how he save her in the jungle of Africa and she was jump by the tiger and drag in the jungle and being eaten up, and she was about to turned the car around and then thought nope... later that night she receive red stem roses from Pete and the card said I make a few mistakes and you mean a lot to me, would you meet me for diner at 8 pm tonight and we can relax and have a glass of red wine.

Then it said Love Pete to Karen and she threw the card and roses on the floor and got undress and took a shower and then went to her bed and put the TV and lay there about half hour and but her mind was on Pete.

She looks at the time and it was late and then she hurried up and got dress and took her car key and lock the door behind her and left and got to her car and got inside and drove to the restaurant and when she got there he was about to leave.

She step in and he was about to step out and then he saw her and he smiled at her and then they both when to the table and they both sat down and he order two steak and red wine and he started to talk to Karen and then Karen listen and then the foods came and they ate and then he touch her hand and then she pull away and then she gave him her hand and then they talked for an while and then Pete said, and he when on his knees and said will you be my wife? He took a diamond ring and everyone was watching and she was stunned and didn't know what to say, before she said yes, I thought that we would first date and then maybe down the road to get married and he said I took too not being with you and I want you and I know that you feel the same.

Everyone was watching and everyone was asking did she say yes.

But Karen was silent and he said please say yes, and she took the ring and place on her finger and he said your saying yes and then they kissed.

When the waitress bought the foods and Pete said I want a bottle of champagne and more roses at the table and she said yes sir, we will bring the roses.

They kissed and kissed and he got up and gave her a hug and hold her tight and Karen kissed him back and after dinner Karen and Pete went into his car and drove around, and then Pete took Karen home and he said can I spend the night with you and Karen nodded her head and said yes, you can.

So he parked the car and they both step out and Karen open the car door, and Pete too, and then they walk to the house and Karen open the house door and they both step inside and she shut the door and he walks toward her and then they kissed and then he pick her up and take her to bed and that night they make love all night long, and then Karen was sleeping in Pete arms and Pete was very near Karen under the cover.

The next morning Karen got up and he was still in bed and she check her cell and no one didn't call her and then Karen took the shower and was getting ready for work and then he woke up and said where are you going and she said to work and why can you just take an day off today?

Well I have a lot of work to catch up but you welcome to stayed, well Pete got up and kissed and convince to stayed home and she said okay I will called my boss and then Karen spoke with her boss and then once again she got undress and they stayed in bed all day long and he also make lunch and they had strawberry and cream and he fed the strawberry to Karen.

Later that day, Karen got up and check the computer and then she said do I need to pick the date and he said sooner the better and so I want to be with you all the times.

Karen just lay bed and the phone rang and she didn't answer and then she said I need to tell my parents that I am marrying you and not your cousin and I think that you should wait to tell your parents about me, but they need to know, I know, but just don't do it today.

Fine and Karen just lay in Pete arms and then Pete said I need to go out for an hour and I will be back and she said fine I will be here.

CHAPTER 37

Karen was about to asked him where he was going but she stops herself and didn't say anything to him. She decided to follow him and but makes sure that he didn't see her, first place he stop at the flower shop and bought red roses and now Karen knew that she had to go back home and make sure that he didn't sees her, and she back up the car headed back home and he knew that she was following him, so he put the roses in the car and then he when for coffee an make a called and said I cannot comes today but I will sees you tomorrow, and then he hung up the phone and drove back home and Karen got home and when into the den room and put on the TV and watched "Bridesmaids and he walks in and he said well you are watching a movie and so here are red roses, that I love you so much, and then he sat next to her and put his arm around her shoulder and kiss her on her lips.

About one hour later he got an called and he took in the bedroom and it was Josh and said why you didn't comes to the shipyard and he said I couldn't come because I been follow by Karen.

I told you that she will be a problem and Pete said I will handle it and don't worry about it.

What are you going to do went she find out that you are still in the business and he said I will manage her and she will listen to me because she is in love with me and I love her and you are lying to her.

I have no choice and she wouldn't understand and you still going to marry her? Yes and you need to keep your mouth shut and Josh said don't worry by time she will figure out what you are doing and then yours going to have killed your wife and it will come down to that, no I won't happen and you are delusion, no I am not and stop saying that's she mean a lot to me.

You think she does and you don't want any other man to have her so you are the highest bidder and when you get bore with her you will find another one.

I don't want to talked nonsense and I just want to be her husband and so where are you taking her on your honeymoon, of course to Africa and we will do an safari and then we will laid in the bed and go to the beach and we will have a fun times.

Does she know where going on your honeymoon? No it will be a surprise and she will be totally surprise and she might be even mad about it. Promise that you will not tell her, I won't.

In two weeks, the wedding and Karen got her dress and veil and her shoes and so Karen hid the wedding gown and Karen said who was that I on the phone and he lies and said it was his mom and then said I need to do some paperwork.

Karen turned off the TV and went to the bedroom and got change and then sat on the bed and pick up a book and started to read and then Pete cell rang and she saw it was Josh, but called him and said you missed a called and he took his cell and text Josh and said don't called me.

Josh text back and said I think she know that I called you, and why are you saying that? I think that she pick up and then it went into voicemail and I hope that she didn't answer, and Pete came to the room and the light was off and Karen was fast asleep and Pete got change and then he went to bed and put his arm around Karen.

The next morning went Karen got up Pete was gone and he left a note and said he had to bring the paperwork to the office and Karen once again fell asleep and about one hour later Karen got up and then when into the shower and then got dressed and when to work.

Karen came to work and said well what should do now, and she said go to the back room and selection the dresses and put them on the rack and prices them and then, you need to do inventory and Karen said that fine I will.

Then the phone rang and Karen answer and it was Josh and he said don't marry my cousin and he is no good, stop this harassment me.

Later that day Karen spoke to Pete and he said not to marry you and you still want him to be your best man? Yes, he will do something to stop this wedding and Pete said he won't.

Why is he's like protecting me from you and what is he up too? I don't have a clue and in two week you will be my wife. Yes I will.

After talking with Pete, Karen got a bit stress and couldn't focus what she was doing and she asked Jessica that she could leave early have an extreme headache and she said yes you can go and I will be fine at the store and Karen said are you sure and she nodded her head and then Karen left.

About half hour later, Josh step inside the store and looks around and Jess came up and said can I help you and then he said, yes you can help me.

CHAPTER 38

Next minute he pointed an gun at her and she said please don't shoot me and I will do what you wants, and he said come closer to me and she did and then he put his hand over her face and then she fell asleep and then he place her on the floor and he search for her car keys and then the store and then stolen about five grand and took her to his car and place her into the trunk and place tape over her mouth and tied her up and close the trunk and lock the door of the dress shop and speed off and went to the boat dock and put on the boat and still tied up and on the bed and then he lock the door and then started up the motor and sped out into the ocean, and he was steering all the way to Africa.

Then he left a message to Pete and said I have a girl for sale and he said who is she and he said it Jessica and he said you fool, you stolen the mob daughter and you are really crazy and yours going to get killed

Stop talking and meet me at the location and Pete said I cannot go with you to delivery her to man that will paid a lot of money, well if the mob find out you will be swimming with the fishes.

Then Pete said I don't want to know, just do it and no detail, do you understand? Yes loud and clear and Pete hung up and then Karen called and said I was trying to reach Jessica and no one answer and Pete said she probably went home, so I will try her cell and Pete said why not?

So Karen tried a few time and it when into voicemail and then left a message and so Karen decided to go back to the store and then she when inside and but didn't see any mess or anything like that's and Karen saw that Jessica left her phone and then she called Pete said something is not right here, what Karen, what wrong? Jessica would never leave her cell and her purse behind I think that she got kidnap and your mind is going into image, no she could be in trouble and Pete said, she probably when out with her boyfriend, but she were not leave her stuff, then Karen hung up the phone on Pete and called the police and they said, how long is she missing, about two hours and so that is too early to be a missing person.

I feel that she is in danger and we need to find her now and then about a minute later, Pete walk in and Karen said, you didn't have comes, but I did and I was worry about you and your friend.

Then she whisper in his ear and said tell me the truth, did Josh kidnap her and Pete said no.

Now Karen told the information and describe how Jessica looks and Karen had a recent photo and hand it over to the police and Pete said she probably just around the corner and she said I know something is not right here and she saw a cigarette on the floor and she said officer, Jessica doesn't smoke and I find one on the floor and he put into a plastic bag and then Pete said I need to go back to the office and I will be back soon and he walk out and make the called to Josh and said are you trying to rude my wedding and he heard a scream and he said got Jessica and you need to bring her back now.

Josh hung up the phone and Pete called and no response.

Now Pete was furious and he didn't want to show it and he went for a walk and called Uncle Steve and said Josh is out of control and you need to tell him to bring that girl back, immediately and we have problem, and he said I know my son is just doing his job but he pick the wrong girl, uncle. She is the boss where Karen work at her shop and Uncle Steve said that was the plan to gets your girlfriend back to Africa and Pete said I took care of that, because Karen and I are going to Africa for our honeymoon, and Uncle Steve said they are sailing to Africa has we are speaking, you mess up plan and now Karen might cancel the wedding and Uncle Steve said, she won't she loved you and I sees it in her eyes and so you have nothing to worry about it.

But why do you want Karen in Africa, well the seller want her and we will deliver and Pete said I am not going to hand over my wife to him and not even if you paid you five millions.

No, so I should cancel the trip and his uncle said don't double cross me, nephew, I am not going to give her away, and I love her, but you love money more., that is not true.

Meanwhile on the boat, and they would sailings along and then Jessica said to Josh know what yours up too

Josh said yeah, I am going to sell you to the highest bidder, you can, what are you saying, that yours uncle and my uncle work together and he cannot sell his niece. So you got wrong girl and then Josh kissed her and said, yeah, yours right, you want Karen and she is a high price girl.

Then Jessica said well Pete won't let her go and I just seen it in his eyes and he is in love with her. Well you smart Jessica and then they heard a boom.

CHAPTER 39

One minute later they were in the water and Jessica was calling out to Josh and she couldn't see him and then she saw those sharks coming toward her and Josh just came above and said don't move just be quiet.

At that point Josh and Jessica was surround by white shark and they were getting closer and closer and Jessica started to move her legs and Josh said don't make any movement and then it felt her leg and now Jessica was in panic and Josh was about to swim to Jessica, but then Jessica said don't move there is an shark behind you and he didn't hears what she said, and about a minute later, he got pull down and Jessica manage to climb up to a wood panel and sat there and one minute later, she saw blood in the water, and Jessica remember that she had an cell in her pocket and she was going to try to see it if would work, and at the moment, nothing and she was surrounded by sharks and holding on tight and no signal on her cell, and then she drop it in the water and she started to cried and had to think fast to get the cell back and but she couldn't reach it and she just sat there.

Meanwhile Uncle Steve called Josh and nothing and he thought well he is busy and then thought he was supposed to contact me and he didn't and I believe something is wrong and then Karen walk in and said what did you do with my friend and boss that I work with and Uncle Steve said I don't know what you are saying.

Then he left and Pete said come here and I do not keep secrets from you Karen, if you are you need to tell me now, and Pete said I am not lying.

Now Karen was getting angry and furious at Pete and I think I cannot go through with the wedding and Pete said I love you and I love you too.

Then Pete calm Karen down and they kissed and they make love.

Karen said are really telling me the truth and I can I really trust you Pete? He nodded his head and yes you can.

Meanwhile Jessica was afraid that they might tip down fall into the water and luckily, a boat came and she was her Uncle Tony, and he said what the heck are you doing out here, asked your friend Steve, and if Steve had something with this I will fix his ass and kick, and Jessica said I am glad that you came and he said well we need to sail to Africa and we do have a blonde hair girl and he is about 5 feet and 3 inches and they are paying a fortune.

So you pick up the girl I told you about? Yes and she is the right fit and we will get a bundle and then you don't need to work at your dress shop, uncle that where I find out and pick out the right girl and then you grab them and sell them, okay that you cover and no one except me and I find the target for you.

Yes you are a good niece and you work well with the family business.

Thanks Uncle and I will go to the deck and check out the girl and she probably figure out I set her up, if she give you trouble, you shut her up but don't damage the merchandise, and I won't Uncle.

Jessica peeks and said you will be sold and we will become a sex slave and you will obey your master, because you don't have any manner.

About ten day they sold the girl and then Jessica was headed back home with five million in suitcase and she kept it very close to her and then she boarded the plane in Africa and the plane was headed to Miami and Karen was going to leave Miami and move back to Manhattan and so she decided if Pete has to be in the business to protection the family she will keep quiet and she doesn't want any threaten from his family, and they do come through hurting Peoples.

Karen mind is just getting married to Pete and go on a safari with Pete and then settle down in Manhattan and work at the job that she had before and Pete said hope that they will take you back, and she I hope so.

About two weeks from now there will be an wedding between Pete and Karen and they send out the invitation and they have the hotel in Manhattan, the Marriott hotel near Time square.

Now Karen is getting the fitting for her wedding gown with silk and pearl and satin and veil and white shoes and her mom will have a blue dress and some pearl on top, and matching shoes and then Karen got the called from Jessica and Jessica said I am coming home and first thing that Karen asked how is Josh? I don't know, so who is he? You met him I am not sure if I did, so tell me how he looks well not now I am at the bridal shop, so I will chat with you later. Then Karen hung up the phone and Jessica got a bit pissed that Karen hung up on her and then she just put her cell away and walks into her seat and waited for the plane to go on the runaway, and takes off.

Karen was like wow, don't I looks good in that dress and her maid of honor said yes you do and Pete will adore and will want to take off your dress after you get married and go on your honeymoon and said saying that you mean the night of in the bridal suite, has husband and wife, yes.

CHAPTER 40

About one hour later Karen got her dress and her mom and the bridesmaid and they carried them out and Karen said why don't we go out for dinner at that Italian restaurant and one of bridesmaid, said well I prefer to have steak, and bake potatoes and Karen said I am carving for pasta and with tomatoes and basil.

But Karen mom said well I will be going home and cook dinner for your dad and Karen said mom, why are you leaving and I want you too stayed, I will called dad and tell him that you will be late, and Karen mom said don't do that he will be angry and so I will talked with you later.

Then about a minute later, Pete called and said, I am in the neighborhood and can I join you girls? Wait a minute, and Karen asked and they said why not!

About ten minute later Pete arrival in the cab and they went to Gino and the girl were at the round table and Pete join them.

Before he sat down he kissed Karen and said "I Love you".

Then he sat next to her and then they order pasta and Pete order Shrimp and pasta and order wine.

They started to eat and then Pete got a called and he had to leave and he just got in hurried and didn't even said goodbye and ran out.

About four hour later he called Karen said that his cousin was found in the ocean and he got killed by a white shark and he is in the morgue.

Karen said should come with you and he said no I will do it myself and then I said I love you, and I will see you later and then hung up the phone.

Five day later was the funeral and Pete and his family and Karen next to him and they were in tears and Pete was very upset and blame it in Jessica fault and she was the one that killed him, and Jessica walk into the church and Pete started to yelled and scream at her and said it is your fault and she said I tried to save him and I couldn't, but you left him in the ocean and you didn't report it to the authority, you just left the country with Uncle Steve.

Yes I did and I had no choice and Pete said you could call someone and she said I did but my cell didn't work, then your Uncle Steve came and took you.

Yes and I just did my job and came back and I found out that they found the body pieces. Because the shark bitten him in half, and then he just kept quiet and then the mass started and they all stood and then sat and sang song and then the mass was over and Pete was one pall bearer carry the Casket.

Karen was in back and she was looking at Jessica and Jessica was like a cold person and didn't recognize her and she was like, Karen came up to her and said tell me what were you were doing with Josh in the first place?

WELL ASKED YOUR BOYFRIEND, I will and she said I will tell you what happen at the dress shop and you will not believe me, I probably know what happen it did happen to me.

So we will chat later and we should go for drinks and Karen said not today but maybe today and she said you need to have fun before you get married.

I know what you are saying, but I need to be with Pete tonight.

Jessica just got up and left and Pete said what is she's causing trouble between us no and everything is fine, are you sure? Yes!

A week from day and the wedding, so can both control yourself and that I can have peaceful wedding Uncle Steve, and Jessica, and don't ruin my life, and Karen mean a lot to me and I want her to be my wife, and then they were silent and Uncle Steve does Karen know that Jessica is your first cousin, no and we will not tell her, fine, that good to know and so Pete just walk out of the room and was looking for Karen but she left and Pete was about to called her but stayed with Jessica and Uncle and discuss the business and what deal that he make to protection Karen and her family and then he was relief that no harm would against them and then he said so I will be going to home now, and don't have anything else to discuss, no and then got his jacket and walks out and shut the door and then Jessica said we will have a problem with your nephew, I can sees it and Uncle Steve said don't jump to conclusion and I am not but I see it.

I think you cause the problem and so I think after the wedding we maneuver the girl into the boxes and shipped them to the master mind that sell the girl and we will get ours money before shipping them and that was the deal and bargain, I like how you think, uncle.

Later that night Pete got home and Karen was in bed and sleeping and Pete was very quiet and got into bed and kissed her forehead and then lay his head on the pillow and fell asleep.

CHAPTER 41

Day of before the wedding and Pete was a wreck and he when out with his buddy and got drunk and high on cocaine and didn't show up for the day before wedding dinner and Karen called and he cell when to voicemail and now she was worry if he was going to show up and then Jessica saw his phone ring and she took off the sound and got close to Pete and then she went into his bed.

When he woke up she was next to him and naked and Pete said what are you doing cousin? Well I thought you were paid attention to me.

Your my cousin and get out of bed and get dress and then he saw his cell 10 miss called and he said what have you done, are trying to sabotage my wedding you bitch, she is not worthy of you and you should married someone the family that want the same has you and Pete said that Karen wanted the same has I do and don't do this again and I will tell Uncle Steve about what you did, and Jessica said Uncle Steve, does not trust her and she will betray you.

You don't know that's do you? Yes, she is not like us and she will get the business and ruin it for the family and we will end up in prison.

Pete said you are delusion and I want to get out of here now and Pete got up and when into the shower and Jessica try to sneak in and he close the door and said leave now and I need to called Karen and apology that I was a fool of getting drunk and high and she is not the one for you.

Get out now, and he slam the door and got into the shower and then his phone rang and it was Karen and he answer and said I am sorry that I didn't show up for the dinner and Karen said I know, you got cold feet and a bit afraid of getting married.

No, I was stupid and I was not thinking and so I will sober up and comes over and Karen said the night before the wedding you will sleep in your own bed and Pete said why can we just be together, and Karen said well I am a little old fashion and so I will see you tomorrow at the church of Saint Mary. The wedding at 10 am and don't be late, and he said I won't Karen, I love you too much.

Tonight Pete when to his parent home and to his bedroom and got his suit on the door and his brother came in and said, I thought that you were be staying with Karen, but she told me that she will be with her maid of honor and bridesmaid and so I said okay and then Pete put on the alarm and when to sleep and but he couldn't sleep and then he close his eyes and fell asleep and meanwhile Karen was pacing back and forward and she was a wreck and she knew that she was going to have a family that might end up prison and she was a bit worry but she didn't talk about it and so then she got the white silk, lace, pearl long gown on the door and then she said to the maid of honor where are my shoes and she started to yelled and scream, and like a crazy woman.

Kelly said to Karen, I found your shoes and I got you something blue and I got a old antique necklace and I think that you will like it, and she looks it and it was your mother and Karen said I cannot wear it, and she said my mom were love that if would wear it.

Then the phone rang and it was Jessica and said you should just not go through the wedding what are you saying, I thought you were my best friend and it sound like you hate me, and she said I don't hate you but Pete is not the one that you should married.

Karen said I am enough nerve and now you are stressing me out and Karen hung up the phone just flop into bed and Kelly said you cannot go to bed with your wedding dress, and then Kelly just walk out of the room and when into the kitchen to get a glass of water.

Kelly got the water and then when back into the room and Karen was fast asleep and then Kelly just sat on the chair and then fell asleep and Kelly forgot to put on the alarm.

The next morning, day of the wedding and Karen looks at the time and it was 9:45 am and the wedding was at 10 am and then Karen when to Kelly and said get up and we need to go now, and Kelly said, we are not late.

Then Kelly looks at the clock and said shit we are going to be late, and then the limo driver rang the doorbell and now Kelly and Karen were rushing and Karen said where are my shoes and they are under the bed and Karen bend down and find them and just left the necklace and they close the door and left.

They got into the limo and Kelly said I am so, so sorry, Karen for getting late up and Karen said be quiet I have a headache.

All the ways to church and Kelly was searching for the veil and her dad was waited outside for Karen to come, and walk her down the aisle and Karen just jump of the limo and put on her shoes and veil over her face.

Meanwhile Pete was at the alter and waited and waited then SAW Karen.

CHAPTER 42

First the maid of honor with blue silk dress and pink roses in their hands, and then the bridesmaid follow with light silk dress and two pink roses in their hands and the flower girl with yellow dress with pink flowers, and white shoes and curly hair.

Pete standing and then Karen and her dad walks down the aisle and he smiled at her, and the music playing. Now Karen walk down the aisle and Pete standing next to the priest and Pete has a white rose on his suit and everyone is looking at her and she had tears in her eyes and she know that she really love that man and then her father walks up to the alter and his hand to Pete and said I am giving you my daughter and then her father sit down next to his wife and hold her hand the ceremony begins and Pete repeat what the priest is saying and Jessica walk in and sit in the back of the church and then Uncle Steve walk in and the door slams and but they still continue and then the priest says you are husband and wife and you can kiss your wife and they kissed and they both walk down the aisle and everyone throw rice and then they when outside and they went right into the limo and left.

Karen said why didn't we wait for my parents to comes out, we will sees them at the hotel at the restaurant, and she said your right and they kissed and then they got there a bit early and they sat in the car and Karen was unbutton his shirt and he was unzipped her dress and but someone honk the horn at them and Jessica said wait until yours on your honeymoon and Karen said butt out and you make me sick, and she said I could have him, and Pete said never.

Jessica said I will sees you inside and Karen said sure and then Karen parents came and said, we will see you inside and Karen and Pete said well we have to go inside and she said my can we just leave on our honeymoon, well our flight is until tomorrow, and she said we are going to Africa?

Yes and we will love it and she said I hate the wildness and I like being in the city and not in some jungle and he said remember you and I agree that we are going, yes I do and I don't like it at all, and don't be such a bitch.

At that moment she felt like slapping his face but he just hold it back and kissed her hold her tight.

Then he let her go and they steps out of the car and walks inside and everyone looks and then they introduce them Mr. and Mrs. Pete Snow.

They walk to the table and then they sat and then everyone make sound with their silverware and they kissed and pictures were taken and then the music began and Pete and Karen first dance has husband and wife and then the parents join in and then they had a cake and Pete cut a slice of cake and fed it Karen and then Karen fed to Pete.

Music was playing and Karen had a couple glasses of champagne and started to be silly and started to talk about her husband and then Uncle Steve came up and said take her out now before she blur out something and so Pete take her out and Karen started yelling and screaming and all the guests are gossip about the Karen and then Karen parents said, listens my daughter's when a through a lot hell and back now she got a little drunk, come on what kind of peoples are you. Then the dinner was over and the guest when home and meanwhile Karen and Pete were in the honeymoon suite and Karen said I don't want you to control me, but you were drunk and I had to get you out of there because you were acting crazy, thanks a lot hubby. Then she got up and vomit in the bathroom and she got up and then said shit I rude my dress, and now I have to take to the cleaner, but maybe your mom can take it.

Tomorrow we are going to Africa, I know, don't reminder me about our honeymoon, and then fell asleep in his arms. Meanwhile Pete get up and make a phone called and makes sure that Karen is fast asleep and called Jessica and said. So do we have the a package to deliver tomorrow and she answer yes and you are taking an private jet to Africa and I will be on the commercial flight with Uncle Steve, we will be using your ticket, you know that Karen will be mad and furious about going on the private Jet, I know and you don't have tell me, so what is she doing, now, she is sleeping, are you sure and she is not listening what you are saying, no…

About ten minute later Pete when back to sleep and somehow Karen woke up and looks around and but Pete was asleep and so she put her head on the pillow and then Pete got up and went to the bathroom and check his cell and no called and he had a gut feeling about the private jet.

Because they will have the girl that they will sell and Karen is totally against his family business and Karen is afraid that they will get caught and once there was a time that Karen was the victim and she didn't know how to help.

The next morning Karen got up and when to take a shower and then saws his phone blinking and so she check the message and listen to it and then she was quiet and angry at the same time and but kept quiet and delete the message from Jessica.

CHAPTER 43

So Pete and Karen were on their way to the airport and she was wandering if her husband would tell her about the change of plan and if he was going to be honest and but Karen just kept quiet and bit her tongue.

Karen knew that she has to stand up and tell her husband how she felt about his work and she doesn't like it at all.

When they step into the limo and then they sat very close and then he put on the radio really loud and told her to listen and she nodded her head and then she wrote something on the piece of paper and she said I think that we are being watched and he said yes, but Jessica and Uncle Steve.

Then she written said will you ever going to get out of the business and he smiled and said it going to happen tonight and then the limo speed out of the parking space and headed to Kennedy Airport to gate 322 and the package will be there and she said, it will be delay for 30 minutes, you receive a message from Jessica and go to storage 34 and it will be there.

I am scare and we will get caught and we will end up in prison, no we will not I got that cover and what do you mean, I cannot says more and then he turned off the radio and wrote and said just follow my lead, you are not telling me everything, I can, they are listening to us.

Then he grab her and hold her tight and then unbutton her blouse and she unbutton his shirt and she took it off and she was in her bra and he was about to remove the bra and then the phone rang and Pete just listen and didn't speak and Karen said who was that's?

But Pete was silent and not a word from his mouth and then the limo went to terminal B and then the car was park and they got out and they walks through security and then they got to the plane and a girl was in her seat and she was about 18 year old and she was tied and Karen said I should untied her and he said no, we need to go through this and make no problem, then tried to whisper in her ear and but he stop himself and because he knew someone was watching him and so he just sat back and buckle seat belt. And he said to Karen, do the same and it will be lift off in few minute and then he wrote a message in a code and now Karen was quiet and then the plane was on the runaway and so then they when up and Karen said can I speak now, and he put a radio on loud and now you can speak and so can I.

Karen asked her name and she said it was Valerie and she is from Boston and she was on a date and then I was drugged, and Karen said I do understand, I went through that kind of situation myself, I know what you are saying captain came out and it was Uncle Steve and Pete was surprise and then Jessica came out from the plane, and Pete said what are you both doing here? Well we don't trust you so we came aboard and so we will be together, and Karen said I knew it, from the start, and Uncle Steve said why don't you shut your wife up for once, don't tell me what I have to do with my wife and don't put a hand on her, so what are you going to do? Shoot me?

So we all died, Karen kept quiet but there was going to be a fight but then Uncle Steve said I need to fly the plane and right now it is on autopilot.

Pete went in the front and started to speak to his uncle and said why did you bring Jessica and don't you know that she is trouble, yes but also good planner, so what does that mean?

At that moment Valerie was trying to untied herself and Jessica pointed a gun at her and said if you tried to escape, you will get a bullet in the head and Valerie said I just want my hands to be free and I am not going to jump off from 50 thousand feet, then Karen went to Valerie and untied her hands and gave her water and some foods and Jessica was watching and looking at both of them seem like Jessica was trigger happy and Karen said just sit quiet and you will be fine, thanks!

Now it is about two hour later and they are getting closer to the destination and Valerie was very nervous and quietly begged Karen to help her and Karen said didn't says anything just watched, and then Valerie started to cried and then Karen try to give her a hug and but Jessica pointed the gun and said sit down Karen, so am I hostage too?

You think that Pete got married to you because he loves you? Karen said yes he does love me and she said yes because you will make him rich, what?

Then Pete came back to the seat and Karen nicely asked him, are you going to sell me? He pause for a minute and said no I am not, who put this nonsense in your mind, and then he looks at Jessica and said don't listen to that troublemaker, and Karen said I won't.

I cannot wait to go on the safari with you Pete and it will be an wonderful time, sure it will be.

Less than a minute they are about to land and Pete wink his eyes.

CHAPTER 44

Now Karen knew that it is in motion and need to distracted Jessica and Uncle Steve and Karen was going to keep them and Pete and Valerie would going to leave the plane but Pete gave Karen a weapon and if they make a move, her order to shoot, and Valerie was relief and started to thank them and Pete said don't thanks me, I need to get you on the American Airline and it will take you back home, but Pete didn't know it was a set up and then Karen and Pete was tied up and tape over there mouth and it was really tight and Karen said thanks a lot now we are in big trouble, no kidding, I thought she was a victim but she was just a setup and it is big time, and then Jessica said back home your parents will hostage and you will do what you says, if you don't I will give a order to kill them.

Please don't I will do what you say and Valerie walk them out of the plane into the terminal and the buyer was there and he said this must be Karen?

Karen said I am not going with you and he laughed and said, well do you want your mom and dad get a bullet in there head? Yours going to killed them, anyways, and I am not going and then Pete said go with him and Jessica came up and kissed him on the lips and they both left. Before Pete left he wink at Karen and she knew that she were be safe, and about a mile away he when up to Uncle Steve and Jessica and Valerie and said where is he taken her? But they refuse to speak and then Pete pointed the gun at Valerie and he said I will shoot you and you will died, and Valerie blurred out and said taken her too "Cape Town" and push her down to the floor and Pete fled and Jessica and Uncle Steve slapped her and took her away and said yours going to paid.

It his wife and you stole her to the highest bidder and that was wrong and not the boss and now yours going, but you won't be seen again, so yours going to killed me? Yes and we should have done this a long time ago and you just not loyalty to the family, are you? Yes I am and be quiet and she put on the silencer on her gun and fired the shot and Valerie was dead, and they took a plastic bag and put her inside and dump her on the side of the road to Cape town.

Later that day, Pete know the location where girls were bought so he just drove in and then snuck inside and he saw Karen sitting and getting prepare to be the seller slave, so he somehow make her notice him and she just sat there and didn't make a sound and then he saw the seller and he when up to him and he knock him out and untied Karen and ran out and jump into the blue car was park and start up the engine and drove off and Karen said you save me but we need to get to the hotel and go on the safari and Karen said is that a good idea, because they won't except it, good thinking…

Meanwhile Jessica and Uncle Steve left Africa and headed back to Manhattan and two thugs came up and said yours not leaving, and one of them said the deal when sour and you got the money and we want it back, and Jessica said, well we didn't stop the sale and we gave him the girl and leave us alone.

No, give us the money now and then the gun when off and miss Jessica by an inch and she said Uncle give him the money and I don't want to died here.

So Pete and Karen got to the hotel and check in and about one hour they were on the safari and Karen said well I am seeing elephants and tigers and lions and wild cats and she said do you know that there are bats they fly at night in Africa? I didn't know that's and then they got into the white jeep and there were more in the jungle and deeper and deeper and she said we will not be stranded in the jungle and he said no, but we will have camp tonight and then we will sees the waterfalls and mountains and we will ride the river, and she said that sound good and he was taking pictures and of both of them and then he was looking around and about a second later, Karen saw the eye of the tiger and then the tiger jump out of the bush and right on Pete and Pete was gone and now Karen was alone and but the tour guide said, I think that we are not safe in this area so we need to leave now and she said about Pete, and he said sorry for your loss and we don't have much time and we need to go now.

So they got their stuff and then he said be careful of the snakes and she said I know and they reach the river and then they saw a crocodile and she started to run and the tour guide said don't worry Karen we will be fine and said how can we when crocodile are on the ground that we walks on, I will protection you Karen and then Karen said I think I left the water and some foods back at the camp and he said we will be fine, Karen.

So they walks for mile and mile and then they rest and then they continue the journey in the jungle of Africa and it started to get dark and so the tour guide Kenny said now we will set up the camp and then in the morning we will leave, and she said okay fine.

Once again Karen loss a love one and she had tears in her eyes and she didn't want to cried but she did and then she when into her tent and when to sleep and the next morning she was alone and Kenny was gone.

CHAPTER 45

One minute later, she sees Kenny coming back with fishes and a jug of water and she didn't says anything at that moment, and they light the fire and skin the fish and cook over the fire and said, we will be here for one day and then we can climb the mountain and you can get a ride up river has Pete paid for.

Yes, but I really don't want to be here alone without him and I just prefer if we go back to the hotel and tell the authority what happen to Pete.

I really understand Karen but we need to do this safari and your own safety and it been order by Pete to protection you from the bad guys.

So they stayed for two day and then the safari was over and Karen when back to the hotel and pack her stuff and left the hotel and when to the airport and left Africa and when she arrive to Manhattan, Karen had tears in her eyes and then she got into the terminal and she thought she was losing her mind, but she saw Pete standing and waving at her, and now she thought that she was seeing a ghost, and he came up and said "you thought I was dead"? She said yes I thought you were are you real? Then she touched him and said how could you do that do me? Yes the tiger drag me but I got away and I just went to the hotel and I got patch up and I when back home, then she slapped him and she said, I was miserable and lost without you when the tiger took you in the jungle and I thought it ate you up, no I standing here and we need to leave and get home, and she said I am going to my parent home tonight.

She took her suitcases and left and took a cab and Pete just stood there and then ran to her and she was gone. Pete tag a second cab and follow Karen home and tell her that she had a bad dream that a tiger jump at me and so that didn't happen and now she is thinking of Joey and we had a wonderful time in Africa and the safari and I don't why Karen is acting crazy.

About two blocks away from their Karen got out and was like staring blank and confuse and Pete came up and said you had a bad dream and you are not thinking clear, are saying that I am crazy? No but you are a bit confuse and thought that I was jump by the tiger, would you? No, don't you remember the boat ride and seeing elephants and monkey and lions and tigers, but it was at like a zoo, they were cage in and so, you got bit paranoid, sorry.

Then they got close and Karen said I thought you were dead, no don't you remember that we escape from Uncle Steve and Jessica and we had a good journey and so now we are home and we will start a new life.

Then they got to the door and Karen had her suitcase and Pete was carry his and she said I am glad to be home with you and then the door open and Karen and Pete walk inside and then she sat down on the couch and Pete went into the other room and Karen called out no one didn't answered.

The next morning Karen got up and she was alone and she looks around and said probably Pete when to work.

Then the phone ring and it was her mom and said how was Africa, Karen said it was good and then her mom said sorry that you loss Pete to the tiger, mom what are saying, Pete is home, don't you remember what happen? Yes he is fine. Two days honeymoon you lose your husband on the safari and it just came out of nowhere and I think it didn't happen and I saw him at the airport and you are delusion and so he is gone and now you must go now. I am tired of being control by everyone so, mom just leave me alone and I will survive this, I done that before with Joey and now I can do it with Pete.

137

So I will stayed in Manhattan, and I will change job and I will live in the same place that Pete and I found and I will go out with my friends and I will not be negative and I will be positive and I will do it, do you hear what I am saying, yes and then she hung up the phone and unpacked and but they never found the body of Pete, and time went by and Karen grow stronger and felt that she can do anything that she wants.

One day Karen got a called from one of the police said they did found torn pieces body and no Identity and she said I will fly to Africa and sees if it Pete.

So Karen got herself a puppy but took it to her mom when once again that she left to Africa and her mom and dad wanted to stops her but she didn't listen and so she left and came back in ten day later and it was not Pete.

Then Karen decided to take time off and just go on a mini vacation and so she when to Atlantic City and she stayed for one week and met a guy name Brian and got married at the justice of peace and they gambling a bit but stayed in bed a lot and then he tried to tell her what to do and she stood up and said I want to says something but I bit my tongue and I decided not to say anything right now, but then Karen change her mind and said, don't boss me around, do you hear what I am saying and I am not your property, but your wife. Then Brian said, okay, okay!!!

Later that night they make passion love and in her eyes she saw Peter and he said, what wrong and she said nothing and just kiss me, and they kissed.

CHAPTER 46

They make love and she said, I love you and he said I love you too!

Promise that you won't me leave and Brian said, no you are my life and I want to be with you all the times.

Then they hold each other in bed and they talk and he said he lost his wife Joan, about 6 month ago and I thought I would never love again, and you walk in and I knew it was you, and I felt the same about.

About one hour later they were fast asleep and the morning came and Brian gave her some coffee and some breakfast in bed and he join her.

She looks at the time and said, well we have a big decision where to live and he said, I will move to Manhattan, with you and she said I will be very happy that you want to move into the apartment in Manhattan, and he said why not?

Then she explains and said this place was temporary Pete and mine, and he said that okay with me, and that doesn't change anything and then she asked what he does for work and he said import and export and I travel a lot and she said that is fine with me and then he said you can meet my family and she said not today, and he said next week at the Hampton, and she smiles and said okay with me.

Time when by and now they are headed to Manhattan and Brian said, I will needs to move my stuff in and I will have comes back to

Atlantic city and Karen said I can help if you want and he said no I will have moving and so that will be taking care of, and we can spend sometimes and I would like that with my new husband and we can take a ride in Central park and so we just could have more time, I love it, so you will need to meet my parents.

It will have to be after I go to trip to Hawaii and then to Japan and I will be back in two weeks, will that we okay with you.

Sure, no rush and so, and then he said would you like to go with me and she said, well I think that I will stayed home and wait for you too comes home and I just can just leave my job and he said I do understand.

Then Brian got the called and he said I won't be long and so and meanwhile Karen got her stuff out the suitcase and put into the bedroom and but still having vision of Pete at the doorway of the bedroom.

But Brian was speaking with someone over two hours and then he said I got to go to the office, there is a problem.

Karen just sat on the bed and thought well, Brian is very important to me and I cannot be overprotection and so I will bite my tongue and wipe off the dust and then I will go to work and then I will go to my parents and then I will go clothes shopping and get my hair done and I will be fine once again!!!

That night Karen decided to change her life and will tell all book about her life and Karen will title it (ROAR) and she will started writing it tonight and she will not be control even though that Brian is a good man, but she is our person and think on her own and that all it count and she will tell her parents that she will write the book and but she has a feeling that they won't like it and she doesn't care at this moment of her life.

About one hour later Brian called and she said that she is working on a project and he asked what kind of project and she said I am working on a novel and he said, so you will write about your safari and how you survive the jungle and barley with foods and water and how you almost fell in quicksand, no but the tour guide did.

Yes, now I remember what you told me so I will be busy for few hours and so I will be at the conference and so you will not be able to reach me.

Then Karen said well I will be working all night and then I will go to sleep and she said, I feel alone without you, Brian, wish that you would be here.

Then Karen saw a shadow and she thought that she was losing her mind but the lights were coming from the cars that were passing by.

Then Karen sat down near her computer and started to type it out and then she stop and thought well I need to think what actually happen in the jungle with Joey and it was really fast and he was gone.

I just saw his face and then was gone and so my first loss was Joey and then it was Pete and now I am married to Brian. I cannot describe what happen but it just jump out and grab Joey and drag him away, and it was a nightmare and I was left alone. That night I cried for him and I was afraid that tiger would come back to get me but it didn't come back and I was relief and but not safe and I had fish and hunt for foods, and I was scare and terrify and it was one experience that I would like to forget, but I cannot forget Joey and Pete.

Joey was my first love and Pete was the one save me.

CHAPTER 47

I will never forget the two men that love me and cherish me with love.

But there was a time that they tried to control, just like Joey that wanted me to go on the safari and I was not too thrilled, but I went because I wanted to be with my love and I didn't wanted stayed home alone.

When we arrival to Africa, I looks around and they looked at us and I was a blonde with blue eyes and slim/ medium build and my hair was on my shoulder and his hair was a bit short but with a mustache and he was about 5 feet and 9 inch tall and he was slim and he was in shape, but he didn't tell me what to eat and he just told me what to dress, sometime I did agree with him and sometime I could stood up and told him felt at that time I was not that strong of woman, like I am now. One thing that I won't forget the eye of the tiger and the tiger was so close and at that moment I thought I would be torn into pieces, but I was not, and I am just thinking just being an way and then someone that you love is gone, but one little jump and drag away in front of your eyes and staring at you and but not chasing you, but dragging someone that you love into the jungle and eaten them and I think that tiger was an predator and just want to eat and so he choose Joey and he was gone and then my Pete was target by a tiger, and it might not been the same one but maybe the smell got them both and that why they died in the jungle, and I will never know the answer what occurs and just wander if Joey and I didn't go on that safari he probably would be alive today, but I need to move on and have positive thought and then I would be strong and I will have a good life with Brian, otherwise if I think a lot about what happen, I will go crazy and lose my mind and I will lose Brian.

Time pass by and I am a happy woman in love but the past always get my breathe away, and just know what to do, right now, my man treated well but sometime he tried to control me and I don't like that's!

Maybe I should have waited longer before I married him but I thought well why I should have waited, especially life is too short.

But I when through the married and I will stay the rest of my life with Brian that will never change, and Joey and Pete will be in my heart too.

Then the phone rang and it was Brian said, do you want to meet me in LA and Karen said, no I will be fine and Brian said "Please comes to see me" and Karen said okay, I will and so she pack her bag and left a message to her mom and dad and said I will be away for a week and I will called from LA.

Karen book a flight and got her stuff ready and the shuttle came and took her to the airport and she was headed to Brian and so Karen was excited to sees her husband and it was really crowded at the airport and so she waited until she was going to board her flight, and but Karen was uneasy and didn't have the patience, so Karen when for a drink to calm her down.

But she couldn't believe that she saw Uncle Steve and Jessica at the airport and she kind of hide from them and then she saw them with a 16 years old girl board a flight to Africa and now Karen thought to herself that she need to cancel the flight to LA and take a flight to Africa, and she just went to the desk change her tickets and didn't even called Brian and her parents just boarded the plane to Africa, and Karen had her passport and got into her seat and she was about five rows in back, and slide down on her seat and try not to be notice and then a man with a dark suit sat next her and had sunglass and he looks at her and said, so are you for business or pleasure and Karen, just vacation, and he said, well I am going for business and maybe we can go for a drink and Karen said, no thanks I am fine.

I don't mean on the plane and she said I am not interest and just leave me alone and she closed her eyes and the plane was on the runaway and was about to take off and then the captain spoke and said, well we have mechanical problem so we have to go back to the terminal and they all had to get off and then Karen phone when off and it was Brian and but Karen didn't answer it and then they said need to go to gate 7 and Karen started to walk fast and get into the plane but first had to through security and so Karen when through and everyone was seated and now it was back to the runaway and it was to lift off and now they are in the blue sky.

Then she got an second called, from Brian and she just turned off the phone and got herself a drink of scotch and ice and then laid back and fell asleep and about 6 hours later, the plane was about to land and Karen was not sure what she was going to do, but one thing needed to follow Jessica and Uncle Steve and she knew that she needed to save that teenager from the slave market quick and she knew it were be danger but she didn't care and didn't even think.

They all got off the plane and they all started to walks and Karen was not too far from them but didn't wanted to be seen and Jessica said I think someone is following us and so think I will walk in back of you, Uncle Steve.

CHAPTER 48

Jessica spotted Karen said what are you doing here? Karen said well I am just on vacation and Jessica said where is your new husband? Well he is getting the car and then Jessica said that is a lies, and you are a liar.

No, I am not, and then Jessica called out to her uncle and said we have a slight problem from the past and so I will take care of it, and about a minute later, Jessica pointed the gun behind her back and said you should have stayed in Manhattan, and now yours going to dies. No I am not, Karen said, you will not get away with it and don't understand that peoples will looks for me and they won't be looking for you in Africa.

So you wanted to save that young teen and you will not even save yourself, don't be so sure and meanwhile Karen cell was on and he just dial to Brian and Brian heard everything and he called the authority in Africa and told them that someone kidnapped his wife and she is in danger and so meanwhile Karen just did what Jessica said and they headed to the car and then somehow Karen saw a opportunity and she hit her on the head and she knew that she needed to follow that car that just left and so she got into the CAB, and told the driver to follow and so he did and about half mile Uncle Steve stop at the yellow house and he came out and the teenager with the pink dress and she had brown hair and not to short and was about 5 feet and 4 inch tall and not to slim and had a little make up on and red lipstick and a heel.

Karen step out of the car and took the cab to called the authority and he said, I cannot I will lose my job and about ten minutes later, Jessica was not too far and she inform her uncle that the problem is standing out and he looked out and said to one of his man to go behind her and grab her.

Karen was still outside and then someone snuck in back of her and hit her out cold and then brought her inside and tied her up to the chair and put tape over mouth.

Meanwhile her cell was still on and Brian, heard what was happening and so he said to his meeting that he has to leave on family emergency and so he left to the airport and headed to Africa. To save his wife Karen from those bad peoples and he was looking at his watched and pray to god that he were not be late.

Karen said, you will be sorry that you grab me and you will end up in prison and I will be save from my husband and my cell is being trace and that moment, Uncle Steve took the phone and threw it on the floor and steps on it and now you will not be, don't be so sure that I won't be I will, and you will be sorry what you have done to me do you hear what I am saying? Loud and clear, missy, and I am not a missy, and I do have a name and it is Karen. But the radar was and it was tracking the phone and Brian called in some of his friends from "special force and tracking the location and Brian got the first flight out of LA and boarded a plane Africa and so his friend will meet him in Africa and the plan to get on a helicopter and jump out the helicopter and land at the camp and having rifle, and knives to get out, and save KAREN, and the girl kept and so Brian is ready, and he spoke to his friend in the white house and told him the situation and so Brian got the best five men from the special forces to rescue Karen and the girl that they were sold to the higher bidder of slavery of sex, and so Brian wanted to stop that criminal about ten years ago but they escape and now his wife is capture by them and he has the mean to get them and the loss of his younger sister that was rape and torture and killed by Uncle Steve the head of slavery of sex.

Meanwhile Karen is being beaten up and strip of her clothes and men are started to touch, on her breast and vagina and Karen said stop doing that's and then they continue and chain her up and one of the man, so called Jerry, pull down his pant and underpants and how he is like with his penis against her body and she trying to get herself loose and but he tighten it up and then he touches her breast and suck on it and she scream and Jerry said, you are not going get away, you whore, and she said I am not an whore and about five hours later Brian land in Africa and meet up with his friends and headed to the copter and headed to the camp where Karen is being held and now Brian talk with them and said what is our move, well we fly low and then we all jump out of the copter and then we go on foot and do a surprise attack and then do you have the smoke bombs of course I do, and then with the smoke bomb we just go and the smoke they will not see us and that is the plan and go you have my machine gun and yes I do and we have, they will not know what hit them and so we will make sure that no one doesn't get killed but the bad guys, and then Jerry said, now I will put you on the ground and I will fuck you so hard that you will love it and you will enjoy it and now he strip her totally and then tied her on the ground on an old mattress and got on top of her and was about to go inside and somehow Karen untied herself and kick him the penis and then Jerry slapped her face and hit her twice and then hold her face down to suck on his penis and she spit at him and he pull her hair and she quiet.

Meanwhile the helicopter was like few minutes away from the camp and Brian said now it is time that we jump and do the fireworks and his friends, go now, and they all jump out of the helicopter, and landed about one miles away and they walk and at the camp, that Karen was screaming and he was inside of her and fucking her and she started to cried and he said, you cheap whore, I will fuck you all night long and you will be damage good and you will do what I says, you whore, and I am not a whore and he put a sock in her mouth and she almost choke.

About ten minutes later, you hears gunfire and smoke bomb going off and a lot of shooting and one bad guy fall to the ground and Brian got a bullet near his ear but didn't get hurt and then the shooting was back and forward and Jerry said I need to go and see what going on, and he left Karen laid naked on the mattress and more shooting and more men on the ground and Brian snuck in back of Uncle Steve, and stab him and he fell to the ground and then Jessica came out shooting and they shot her in the head and but they kept on shooting and shooting and there was a fire one of the building and so Brian ran in and got shot in the shoulder and at that time, Karen got unchain and one of the bad guy was holding her and Brian came in and he said, if you wants your woman to live, put on your weapon and Karen said, don't put your gun down and so Brian did and then, Ted shot him and Brian had an others gun and shot him in the head and then Brian got a blanket for Karen and wrapped her around it and said I will be right back and she just said don't go and don't worry I will be okay and then she heard a gun fire and she ran out and Brian was on the ground and said, no don't die on me, and he open his eyes and said, I am fine and rest of buddies came and said, so this is your wife, and he said YES!

ABOUT TEN MINUTES. THEY HEARD A EXPOLSION, and the building blew up and Karen said we need to found those girl that been kidnapped and they need to get back home, and Brian said, I found some clothes for you, and one question he asked, did he assault you, at that moment Karen didn't want to speak, and he said, he has that bastard, and I would killed him again but he is dead.

So Karen told them about the building where the girls were kept and they when inside and the girls were frighten and scare and so Karen spoke to them, was

That's time that she was dress, and a bit beaten face with some scar and cut, and bruises, and very quiet and after the police arrival and they took the girls and Karen gave Brian a hug and said, I knew that you would find me.

CHAPTER 49

Then Brian got close to her and said don't go on that kind of journey on your own and Karen said I promise, I will never do this again in my life, and he said you promise and he gave her a hug and then a kiss and then all his buddies said it is time to take your wife home, and about a minute, later, oh my god, what Karen, do you sees what I see, no, not exactly, I see the eye of the tiger, and just turned around slowly and he did, don't move fast, I won't.

Karen said, I when through hell but you rescue me with your buddies and I could have ended up dead and but I didn't.

About one hour later, they still would in the jungle and the tiger was nears by and Brian was taking pictures and then the helicopter landed and they slowly walk to the copter and they slow got on and about a minute the tiger "roar" and at then it disappear in the jungle and Karen said I will never forget the tiger and I believe that you and buddied are champion and I do love you and he said I love you too.

When they were flying over the camp it was burning and in flame and Brian said this operation is will be finished for good and then he kissed Karen and once again, he asked did he violent you anyway, and now she shook her head and with tears and he said it is not your fault, and I will always love you, and she smiles.

Karen touch his cheek and touch his hair and said I thought I would not see you again but you are here and you rescue me from the bad guys, I owe my life and then she saw some blood from his stomach and Karen said he need a doctor now, we will be Cape town, in twenty minutes, but please hurried.

Then Brian passed out and he is losing too much blood, and one of his friend said, hold it tight and it will stop the bleeding, sure I will, he is the man I love. We will be in five minutes and called for an ambulance and they will be there when we land, and Karen was holding him and said don't die on me now.

He open his eyes and said, I will be with you and then he just pass out and she said hurried up and it will be too late, and then they landed and they took him on the stretcher and into the ambulance and Karen went inside by his side and then they shut the door and drove off in a hurry and they got there and the doctors and nurses and took him into the room and Karen stood out and they were working on him and about half hour later, the doctor came out and said you can see your husband now and she smiles and said thank you and she walk in and he was looking at her and said, honey I will be fine and then she stayed with him and then they told her that they had to examines him and she need to wait outside and she said, can stayed and the doctor said not now.

She step out and they examine him and then she was back into the room and he was fine, and then she hold his hand and said, I will never leave again, and he said is that a promise and she said yes.

Later that day, Karen called her parents and told them what happened and her mom said I am glad that you are fine and how is your husband and she said he is fine and he will get discharge in five days and that how long I will be in Africa and then her mom said what exactly happen in Africa and Karen said I don't want to talked about it now, I am fine and that all that you need to know now.

Don't be snapping with me, and you are my daughter and I was worry about you and you should understand what I am saying, I do but not now, okay Karen.

So we will see you in five days if there a complication with Brian condition it will be longer and so Karen said mom and dad I love you both and then she hung up the phone and when to Brian and hold his hands and one his buddy Ted came in and said I will be here for both of you and she said thank you.

Ted sat down, near Brian and Karen and she talked and asked how did Brian contact you and he was not talkative about it and she said okay I won't pride and I am glad to be alive and then Ted said did Brian tell you what kind of work he does and she said yes import and export, okay, good.

Karen said should I know more about his life and Ted said. In time you will know and you are kind of secretive about Brian, well I cannot say or speak about his life, he had to be open with you and not me, and I am giving the man my respect by not telling you.

Now Ted left and walk out and before he did he shook Brian hand and gave Karen a hug and left.

Karen said can have your cell number and he said Brian has it and so I will see you later and walk to the elevator and step inside and when down.

Then Brian started to speak and he said listen when we get home I have a lot to tell you and she said, I need to know and he said not right now.

Brian was about to yell at her those poacher would have killed you.

CHAPTER 50

You walk into danger situation and promise that you will not do that again and she said, I promise and then he's said come close to me and I want to kiss you, and he kissed her lips, and hold her tight, did you know that they were sex trafficking and Karen said yes I did and you still risk your life, yes, and I would do it again. Then Brian got an urgent called and he said I got to take it and she said you are not going on mission, you just got out of the hospital and Brian said when duty called and I have to go and she said I will go too, and he said it is danger and a lot of shooting and peoples getting killed and she said you almost got killed on this mission, and you need rest and be with me.

So he told them not today but about a two weeks from now I will be available for duty to catch the bad guy of trafficking children and young girl and selling them to the highest bidder and so I need to do this job and I know it very dangerous and I need to save those innocent peoples that end up in slave of sex and they have no ways out and we rescue them, just like we did at the camp and I know and it was partly my fault ended up there and being assault by the pig and so you took care of him with this ordeal behind me and I feel stronger and will go on being stronger and also will go to therapy and so each day I will be better and so, but I need to tell you I still see the "eye of the tiger" and I roar, each time when I sees that bad guys, and I would like to jump them and drag them into the jungle and rip them into pieces, and they were get what they deserve, and Brian said I agree and so you do understand my work.? Sure I do and so I will be working at the dress shop and doing designing and I will make a name for myself, and he said I know that you will and you are strong and positive woman that I fell in love at first sight in Atlantic city and then Karen said you really wanted to get into my pant and you did and then you asked me to be your wife, sure, that what happen.

I should tell you in the past I was a very quiet girl and once I did bite my tongue and so then I fell for some loser and I fell a few times and I was not like this but I just got up and I dust myself off and I suddenly I got stronger and then I got the fire inside and I got stronger and I then I saw the light and then no one could not push me around and I was not anymore push down and I was strong woman and I grew stronger each time, and Brian said I do hear what you are saying and will not be abuse and you will not be rude and tell me what to do and he said, hold on, and I am not that type of man. Now they are headed to the airport and so Karen cannot wait to get back home to Manhattan and Brian, said well we will be back home tomorrow and so we can spend time together and then she asked what was in LA? I really cannot talked about it too you if I did I would have too killed you, and then he said I was joking but I still cannot tell you and it is vital to "top secret" and so they were headed to the airport and then they heard some shooting and he said put your head down and Karen did and he took out a gun and started to shoot and he said we are still in danger and so Karen was not to happy and then the car tried to passed them and she said I know this man, and he is Will, and he belonged to the trafficking and he still want me to sell to the highest bidder and Brian said he is not going to get you and you are my wife, and then the car skidded there car and Karen at that moment got scare and bullets were flying left and right and Karen kept her head down and then more in enforce came and rescue Karen and Brian and then they drove off and they were at the airport and boarded the plane and buckle up the seat belt and the door of plane close and Karen said I will miss Africa and I am not planning to go back, and the plane on the runaway and up they went and now they are up at 50 thousand feet and Karen looking out and was relief that she was going home and the flight attendance asked if she wanted to listen to music and she said yes and she put on her earphone and listen to the song, "ROAR" eye of the tiger and she said to Brian, I am listening to my favorite singer and who is that? Katy Perry, and he said oh I see and what song is playing, ROAR, and it is an awesome song, Brian and do you want to hear it, and Brian said well I am exhaust and he fell asleep and Karen listen to the song and fell asleep in his arms and they arrival landed in Kennedy Airport and got off the plane and took a cab home to Manhattan and Karen said I need to tell my parents that I am home and fine, and he said, they got out the cab and Karen open the door and her whole family were waiting for her and they all gave hugs and kissed and Brian when to take a shower and Karen stayed with her family and Karen told them what happened and she was wrong to follow those peoples and she promise that she were not do again and so Brian stood in the shower and started to have nightmare of killing poacher and trafficking peoples and then stood and came out and took a towel and dry himself and Karen was still shook up about what when down but was afraid to speak about being rape and getting beaten and so they stayed for two hours and then Karen and Brian were in each other arms and then they when to sleep and they make love and the next morning Brian was gone and left a note and said I will be back in two weeks and I love you…

Karen had tears in her eyes and just lay in bed had cover over her head, and was just thinking of Brian. Time when by and no word from Brian, but red roses were send, and it would not signed by whom?